LOST IN THE CAQUETA

MICHAEL J. HOLLAND

Copyright © 2023 Michael J. Holland.

All rights reserved. No part of this book may be
reproduced, stored, or transmitted by any means—
whether auditory, graphic, mechanical, or electronic—
without written permission of both publisher and author,
except in the case of brief excerpts used in critical
articles and reviews. Unauthorized reproduction of any
part of this work is illegal and is punishable by law.

A NOVEL

To my children and grandchildren
Janette, Wendi, Dixon, Derrick
Wesley
Savanah
Berlyn
Lincoln
Winter
Jaxsten
Hatcher
Seven
And my best friend Tim Wible
(the guy on the left of the fish)

CHAPTER

1

I 've been told by so many that I should write a book, and as many times as I've told these stories you would think that it would be easy. It isn't, because it's hard to determine if it even happened at all. Maybe it was just chapters lost from the Matrix, or crazier places and dimensions. Maybe I just dreamed this stuff up in a wild imagination of wanting to be Tarzan. Nah!! True life happenings are crazier than things imagined, and of course fishermen's liberty to exaggerate make it more interesting, but in all honesty, this stuff happened but I just cannot prove it. Of course if you got the money and the bravado to go to the Caqueta River you can check it out yourself. The adventure is what you make of it. Mine was pretty gnarly.

Most of us that live the lives of missionaries and the children of missionaries, are raised in two distinct time frames, before and after. We have to become two people at once sometimes. The one I was, and the one I am. I loved it, I hated it. I wish it hadn't happened, I wish it had never ended. It can be hard not to feel schizophrenic about it.

I want to say right her in the beginning that I will be using "memories" and that they might not be accurate. I am going to change most of the names of people, real or imaginary, so that I don't infringe on anyones rights or dignity or their "memories".

Also to avoid legalities and lawsuits and all that goes with the crazy world we live in I will make this a "Novel" and not a biography so that I can indulge in graphic license and spice the story up. Most of this story is coming from true experiences and things that really happened or places that really exist. I hope you enjoy and if nothing else I can stop making excuses for myself and to others every time they say, "you should write a book."

CHAPTER

2

I t is hot! So hot that your eyes feel like they are going to pop out. So hot that when you bend over to take off your socks, your vision goes down to a dark pin prick, and that "OH! Dang I'm passing out" message goes thru your head. You stare at your arms and see the beads of sweat pop out thru the pores on your skin and you think, your hair is going to fall out.

You suddenly remember every sermon on Hell, you heard at the Camp Meetings, where Sweaty Evangelists, stomped and yelled while your imagination and emotions were held in sway and you could almost smell the sulphuric flames that were just outside the door waiting for your first backsliding mistake or lustful thought, or a glance at the girl in the row ahead of you who's miniskirt was in definite defiance of the Holy rolling doctrine that was being expounded upon. Explanations of how the flames will lick at your body, making the skin pop and bubble yet not burning you up. Your skin doesn't melt by the surrounding heat, yet it feels like it would be pleasurable if it would.

I am talking about the first ten seconds you get off the air conditioned Aero Condor propeller driven airplane and step onto the black tarmac of the Florencia airport, gateway to the jungles in the Department of Caqueta, Colombia. This is the last vestige of civilization and cold Coca-Cola.

Its a real place, it looks like jungle out in the distance, but my mind is telling me its Hell and to look for Devils and piles of molten lava that would explain why I'm burning up alive. I can't be dead, I was alive and only fifteen years old. I hadn't sinned enough to deserve this ending. I had been in church more than anyone I ever knew.

My Mom was a Preacher, fiery, pentecostal, tongue speaking, twirling, bible studying maniac who would never lead us into any place but heaven, yet here I am burning alive.

I didn't know you could fly on a plane and land in hell. I thought you had to die first. The cute

4

stewardess who spoke in Unknown tongues and gave me my first taste of Colombiana, the champagne soda pop of national delight was really a servant of Satan,? how did that happen? The airlines brand name was Satena, it had to be Spanish for Satan Airlines. Mom should have known better, where was her gift of discernment and knowledge? Here we are in the heat of hell and no angels anywhere, to rescue us from evil.

There is a big ball of bright red, out on the horizon, I recognize it as the Sun, bigger than I've ever seen it. It is a big ball of red on a blue horizon. It is the burning season in the jungle, and it creates this haze of smoke that filters the light so you can look directly at the Sun and it has no effect, except to pass thru your eyelids, as you close them to wipe the sweat off. It takes a while to learn to just let it drip, don't touch the pouring drops, the never ending wet, it will be to no avail.

Green is everywhere, the green starts as the blacktop ends, and it goes on, and on till sight ends. It changes tones and hue, it changes sizes and shapes, but it goes as far as I can see, until it swallowed in the red haze of the heat. It's the jungle, the real jungle, not the jungle you read about in books and magazines, and I can smell it. As the sweat drops

5

rolls down the crease of my nose, I smell wet, I feel dank, I see green. I itch, I drip, I wipe, I try to breath the air, but it is so thick, with humidity I can't. I'm drowning on dry land. I feel like the Carp in the ponds at the Golf course where I used to go poaching for trout. The carp would come to the surface in droves, sucking at the water top for scraps of food that people would throw in the water, kind of like a nasty nightmare, sucking, sucking, sucking.

I don't even know what I'm looking at, yet I am aware it is always growing, seeping up out of the ground, oozing out of the pores of the earth, sucking the oxygen out of the air.

I would quickly learn that the jungle is one of the meanest, angriest, harshest places I would ever encounter. I had only experienced jungle in the movies, and Tarzan the Ape Man novels. Those jungles had looked and sounded like a great place. Tarzan ran around in a loin cloth swinging from the vines and living in trees. I owned the whole collection of the "Tarzan" series and it never described the Jungle as Hot, or Mean, or Angry. Here I was standing at the edge of the real thing and I immediately knew I was in danger. You can smell it. The green growth, in its shades and shapes, declaring, I am never going to stop.

I cannot understand the so called environmentalists, "tree huggers". All I know is they have never lived in the environment they proclaim they want to protect, and that is so vital that they think they need to save it. The jungle will take over, and kill you and anything that isn't able to get away. It will save itself, it will exterminate you. It will slowly out grow you and replace you, it will rot you, and remove you. It will change its form over and over again until you give up and let it be.

The green will win, no matter how hard you try to stop it. I spent fifteen years, cutting, digging, chopping and never made a dent in it. All you have to do is leave it alone and it will take over. And the winner is the green, the planet saves itself by enduring and outlasting the human organism and its weakness of mortality.

Mold and Mildew are the subtle forms the jungle uses at first. My clothes begin to take on this black hue as they get wet from the pouring sweat you leak from the minute you are awake. The wetter you get the darker the splotches on your clothes. After a few months my clothes are all one color, Grey. They look like real clothes when they are dry, if they get dry, but once the day progresses and the heat rises, and sweat pours off, they melt into a gray smattered color that takes over, until the cloth finally disintegrates.

My mother, who was not much of a seamstress, keeps adding on fresh pieces of cloth, patch on patch, till nothing but the belt loops are original on the pants. The zipper and the belt loops are good. The belt is gone, sweat and oozed salt, have dried and cracked it into uselessness. You quickly and adroitly learn to weave your new belts out of some leafy plant material, that you learn to dry out and weave in some fashion. Every piece of string you come across is saved and hoarded so you can keep your pants up as you lose the weight and baby fat that you might have had before arriving in the Green. There are very few fat people who live in the jungle. Yes I used the word fat, because obese does not exist in this environment, no one gets to that level. It is impossible to gain weight while sweating gallons of bodily fluids, constantly fanning yourself with your sombrero and swatting at the incessant gnats and winged insects that infest the air and are delighted to find some juicy white kid that is leaking sweet fluids. Your energy loss is an undefinable fact. You cannot ingest enough to keep up with the caloric loss.

By the end of the first year in the jungle my hair has grown thick with mildew. I didn't know why my thin brown hair was getting thick and looking black at noon. Usually the sun bleaches your hair blonde. You wear a big sombrero at all times if you at smart.

The sombrero keeps the sweat out of your eyes, and a few of the thousand things that fall out of trees and sky, off your neck. You can always fan yourself with it, stir the heat around and pretend it is cooling you off, while you sit and sharpen your machete, and chug down a bowl of molasses water. After a while I realized my comb was catching, and tangling as I tried to comb my hair, seemingly more and more resistant to the pull and tug of my combing endeavors.

Finally my newfound jungle friends and tell me the truth. That's mildew!!!, you can't wash it off, you can't get rid of it, you can't kill it. You got to cut it off. I resisted that idea and began to use bleach water to rinse it out. Too late, river water and bleach didn't cut it. It was time for the scissors.

It would have been okay, just to loose the hair, but I then lost my hearing in my left ear. I found my way to the Village clinic, and the Diagnosis was Mildew in the eardrum. I was like NO WAY!!

yep... that stuff rotted my eardrum out. Thank God for Antibiotics and Oxygen Peroxide. My hearing eventually came back, somewhat the less, but now when my grandkids read this they will know what that stuff is, that is growing out of my ears. It's a jungle in there.

CHAPTER

3

~~~~~

The assault on your senses when you arrive in a foreign place is like a shock and awe wartime siege. The smells! the first Sense to be first plastered, bombarded, and forever to be remembered. Certain smells still trigger memories to this day. They will stop me in my tracks, explosions of stumbling proportions.

The Colorado Rocky Mountain High Pines, and the Denver air of my childhood are long forgotten, so crisp a memory, blown clear out of the landscape of my mind. The new stuff is like a jaguar run amok in the pig pen, screeches, screams and grunts,biting, bittersweet smells pour over my sanitized senses and leave paths that will never heal.

The Florencia Open market, is the Nuclear Detonation of nostril plunder. Once experienced, it is never to be forgotten. The tightness of the chest at seeing a beggar with open weeping wounds, a leg swollen twice the size it should be in a purple, angry red color, with arm and cup extended, wet, glassy eyes. A Begging cup extended by a black grimy arm, clutched in twisted fingers with long black fingernails. The fetid sour smell of the black ooze that is in the gutters, that I try to avoid, is not happening. I try to stay on the sticky pavement where dead plant life, shucked off shells, leaves and husks are tossed and layered down, but it is the only option to be able to forge ahead, and even that is limited. You just stick to the path of stomped down litter and decomposing matter that fresh vegetables and live animals leave behind during the marketing process.

I am amazed at the tables and rows and piles of things that I know are food, yet I have never seen, or recognize. As a teenager from Colorado my experience with fruit is apples, oranges and bananas. Here I am terrified at the assortment of unidentifiable things that are being displayed.

This display grabs the nose and never lets go. The Spice lady sitting in her stall, surrounded by open bags of Cumin, Asafran, Pepper, Achiote, are imprinted in my olfactory memory forever. These four powdered substances are the strongest and stay in my memory and overpower the Nostril defense for the rest of my life. One whiff and forty years later, I am standing in the Florencia market place like a twilight zone junkie. Jerked from one location and time zone to another.

The banana guy is the one person that gets our attention right off the bat. My stepfather, who was not the brightest bulb on the planet, but another Tarzan fan, realizes that we are standing in the midst of piles and piles of the biggest bananas on earth. These suckers are twelve to fourteen inches long. They are three inches around in girth, and they are piled six feet tall.

Dad quickly sign languages, to the sales man that he wants one of these monstrous delicacies and whips out some of the new pesos we have obtained and exchanges what seems to be a fair monetary amount.

He shows me, and with a great big smile says, "see this isn't so bad after all, it's the promise land.. instead of grapes we got bananas." He tries to peel it, and finds that it is too tough to peel, not really understanding what he has in his hand is a

13

Plantain, not a Banana. Not to be discouraged by what is a minor difficulty and confusing issue, he whips out his pocket knife and begins to shave the peeling off. The salesman standing there beside me and Step-Dad, is talking a mile a minute in a language we of course, do not understand. He has big black eyes, missing a few teeth, brown leathery skin and is a foot shorter than we are. He is smiling and really talking fast, and seemingly faster, as my Step-Dad, peels this banana and starts to eat it.

Step-Dad comments that the pinkish color is kind of strange, and it doesn't taste right. He goes ahead and eats it because he is not one to waste money.

The little guy keeps jabbering the word "Frito…Frito.." and we repeat after him "Frito.. Frito". It took a few weeks before we realized this did not mean "thank you" or "this is good". Frito is the word for " Fry it! Fry it!!"

I'm sure the rest of his conversation, as we wandered away went a little like, "Man I have seen it all now, that Gringo just ate a raw plantain. He's going to be constipated for a month. Only an animal could do that."

We continue to walk thru the market, not a trash can in sight. We are plodding along on top of six inch deep rubble, garbage, leaves, canvas bags, and of course the ooze that seeps up if one stands to long in one spot.

Some of the fruit is scary looking and has big thorny looking skins. There are mounds of green, red, orange, yellow, and all mixed together with the confusing sounds of salespeople hawking their benefits and savors, in a language we couldn't understand.

We turn at the end of one aisle and end up in the Meat market where a new Nostril Demolition Derby starts. Up and down the aisles are raw, bloody slaughtered animal parts and pieces hanging from hooks. There are flies buzzing everywhere. The salespeople, have blood on their hands, blood on their white smocks, blood on the wooden stumps where they are whacking various pieces of animal parts, with axes, and machetes. They all have this smell about them. A smell that brings a reaction to the back of your throat that is creating a desire to expel the air you cannot avoid breathing. Blood has a very distinct smell. It smacks of oxidation, rust with brown sugar, copper pennies in old moldy socks.

When you turn the corner, where the end of the line of vendors sell yesterdays product, it is beginning to rot, and decay and is deteriorating faster than the sales rate. The poorest of the community come here to buy the meat at discounted values, and learn to appreciate the smell, as it signals it is bargaining time.

I think it is time to head to the next row, where Fish is the next item up for the offering. Now its time to really buck up and see what you're made of. The separation of Men from the Boys occurs here.

When all you ever known of fish is School lunch fish sticks, trout from the Colorado streams and a few thousand ugly carp at the golf course, this was a thing of uncharted territories.

Catfish that are six feet long. Big round fish with spots like leopards. Scaly fish like frying pans, Yellow fish with skin like leather, spotted fish, fish with six inch whiskers, and of course the smell, the smell of water that has been in the sun to long, gone green with algae, dark, gelatinous with bile and things that squirm but shouldn't.

Long John Silvers takeout and Red Lobster have nary a candle to hold in comparison. Not by a long shot, and not a jar of Tatar sauce to be seen.

CHAPTER

4

A m I in heaven or am I in Hell? This question runs thru my mind as I stare at the sights before me. It's still hot as hell, but I am standing in the Main Plaza of Florencia, the little capitol city of Caqueta. I watch as hundreds of teenage girls in the cutest identical miniskirt outfits pour by me on the street, and I wonder? Can heaven be this hot, really?

All of them are girls, literally all of them. They are looking at me and giggling or waving, or both. They are holding hands with each other as they pass me on the street, all of them turning to look at me.

Am I in a dream? I am a slender fifteen yr. old American boy with light brown hair and blue eyes, Me, myself, and I, defects and pimples and all that goes with puberty, I am the center of attention from what appears to be the cherubic host of heaven.

The hell of it is, I cannot communicate a word. I cannot understand a single thing they are saying, nor am I able to express my surprise and delight.

All those black haired, brown eyed, coffee skinned female apparitions have flooded out and around me, and what have I just experienced? The rapturous ending bell of the all girl Catholic Schools. I wasn't Catholic, but I was ready to convert! Evangelicalism be damned! I could repent later if I had too.

There are multiple all female schools in the little town of Florencia, each with its special School uniform, all of them swirling by me, in a flurry of colors. a River of Dark blue, Light blue, Dark purple, Dark Maroon, miniskirts. White blouses, White knee socks, waves of Long Black hair, and all with that same strange bubbly babble, a language I would have given anything to have understood.

I never did see where the boys in town went to school. They must have been sent to purgatory. The idea of no competition in this arena of such magnitude was a breath taking experience.

I would make any excuse I could to get into that town square every day around three o'clock to observe this divine phenomenon.

It was like being the First Man on the Moon. I wanted to yell, "The Gringo has Landed"! I was much taller than they were, and as I stood on the sidewalk, the girls would swirl around me, like a boulder in the middle of a river. The bubbly banter they exchanged, was splashing in my hormone addled head. It sloshed and spattered, slamming my Testosterone levels into overdrive. Gurgling waves of self awareness and pounding heartbeats of lost opportunity. Why, oh why had I never taken Spanish class?

I lived next door to a big Mexican family for years when I was younger, in Englewood, Colorado. They were as poor as we were, and believe me, we were poor. The Mexican kids adopted me and my little brother Pat, and let us eat at their table. Mama and Papa spoke to each other in Spanish and the kids understood them but never spoke it themselves, unless attacked by the other kids in school. They all wore suede pointy toed boots and would fight like a pack of dogs for each other.

They were part of the La Raza club in school and I sure wish I had been invited. I might have been able to at least say something intelligent like, I'm the luckiest gringo in the world, or why am I not a Catholic?

Things got a little better as the weeks followed. The home where mission families stayed was next door to a family that helped us. Our interpreter Rafael, lived there with his sister.

She was friends with a few of the cherubic beings that departed their daily abodes in the town square and wanted to meet in the evenings to study English.

Oh, Delight of delights, when ten of the angelic hosts showed up to have me help with their Grammar and Composition Diagrams.

I had a hard time concentrating. When twin sisters Cecilia and Cenilia showed up, it was like kryptonite. I was unable to move. Identical twins, dark brown, tall and thin, their voices and strange speech, firing away at such a rapid pace. I could only sit and wonder, how had I been so, so stupid, and not studied harder in my English grammar classes.

I could not tell which sister was which. I didn't care which was which. I couldn't pronounce Cecilia or Cenilia, but in my head it sounded just like Cinnamon and I love Cinnamon. Those girls were all smarter than me, and had perfect hand-writing and composition. The problem was not one of them spoke a word of English, Not one word. How can you write perfect English grammar and not speak a word of English.

I can't remember what I wrote to them now after all these years, but you can bet I diagramed the hell out of those papers.

CHAPTER

5

‒ ‒ ‿ ‿ ‿

Florencia is the capitol of the Department of Caqueta pronounced (kaw-key-taw). Departments are like States in the U.S.A. The Dept. of Caqueta sits right on the Equatorial line and at its bottom corner, touches Ecuador, Peru, and Brazil. It is where the headwaters of the Amazon River start and flow from Colombia down into Brazil. The Jungle as we call it, is still many miles away but there are patches of it, right up to the city limits. Most of the surrounding miles have been cut down and planted in grass to raise cattle. What isn't jungle, grass or crops is swampland, or Mountain sides to steep to work. The Caqueta is to hot and humid for coffee. You can grow it but it doesn't do very well compared the more temperate parts of Colombia. In fact the Caqueta is to hot and humid for almost everything, but that doesn't stop the populace from trying. It was almost like a glove thrown down in combative defiance, in the face of us Americans that believe we can do anything. We were there to prove to the world that we could survive the End of the World apocalypse, and save souls at the same time.

No joke, that was the plan, my parents had but I, was not really to interested in the plan at that time. I was wondering how to become a Spanish speaking Catholic playboy, or something close to that after witnessing the three o'clock daily rush of angelic hosts. It was a short lived interest because when you get close to the jungle you get introduced to survival of the fittest Theory by degrees you never see in any Tarzan series. Our lives began to take on dimensions and skills that were to say the least extraordinary.

My stepdad was an uncoordinated guy. He was gangly, goofy and just a plain dude. Lots of hair on his back, not much on his head, lots on his knuckles and hands.

He had been a Navy sailor, seen a little of the world, been a jack of all trades, kinda guy. He was looking forward to playing Tarzan of the Jungle

23

more than I was, but hey what guy doesn't look forward to living in a tree house.

We had been told by some of the people already living I the jungle at the Mission, to buy a few tools, especially some new machetes. We had no idea what lay in store for us in the jungle, but it sounded cool. Everyone we saw walking around, was carrying one on their belts, so off we went to the Florencia Plaza. Of course I was not one to quarrel, especially if it took us there at that wonderful three o'clock time frame.

Buying a new machete is like buying a new sports car in Las Angeles. You go from store to store, and you scope them out, some are bright silver, some are dull grey, some are long, some are short, some are curved. You can get fancy colorful, beaded cases for them with long leather braids, or just plain dull heavy leather. That smell of new fresh leather, the chemical odor of Metal and machismo, Decisions, Decisions. Our guide gave us a quick lesson on machete testing. You take the machete in one hand, and with the other you bend it to almost a 90 degree angle. You clip your thumbnail on it and the let it spring back into the straight position. If the machete sings with a crisp long ring, you have a good one. If if

24

stays bent, or just thunks, it's a dud. They have a dozen different names for them too. 'PENIA", "LON DONYO", "AGUILA" "RRULA", Yes, you have to roll that double R. We settled on middle of the road style. Twenty two inches of bright silver steel AGUILA and two metal files to keep them sharp. After a few days of sporting them around and filing them into a semblance of sharp which we were to learn later, that we had a lot to learn about sharp, we proudly decided we were really beginning to get this machete thing down, as we strutted down the streets the plaza with our swashbuckling appendages.

One night it was time to hit the hay, it was hot, humid, and we were really worn out. My brother Patrick and I had to share a bed, under a green army mosquito net that made the bed space even hotter and more humid. It provoked a lot of fights between the two of us. My parents, had to share a bed, next to ours, and it probably provoked a lot fights between the two of them. They were pretty discreet about it though, and it was just the circumstances. The house was small and Gringos and their Gringo beds were big, so unfortunately for Mom and Dad it was tough. You get one room and you make do, with the tight quarters.

Dad came out ready for bed, sporting tidy whiteys, hairy chest, back, and knuckles. No big deal, Me and Pat are bunked down, tugging at the hot muggy sheets and mosquito net, pushing and fighting for space supremacy. Mom comes trundling out in her little sleeping moo moo ready for a sweet repose. Suddenly she lets out a screaming shriek, that makes all Dads hair stand up just like the Wolfman on a full moon night.

There is a spider the size of a big fist, hanging on the wall. Now Dads hair is in full bloom Navaho mohawk. He grabs that new 22 inch machete and as he flies about in tidy whiteys, the swirling dervish dance of the Mad Russian commences. Pinging concrete and Paint Chips fly in all directions, shrieks and screams as Mama in MooMoo, directs the action scene in the new production of Tarzan vs. the Monster Spider. If you have ever seen spiders under attack they are marvels of science. They can move and jump incredible distances and at speeds that defy gravity. Dad not to be outdone also could move pretty fast. He never did touch that spider, not for lack of swinging, slashing and giving his best at Tarzan yodels, and we never did go to sleep that night.

It was impossible to sleep, either out of fear of being eaten alive by the critters, or of being beaten

by Dad for laughing under the covers at his coura-
geous effort in futility. Lesson learned, leave the
spiders alone, they just want to be left alone and
do not like dancing gringos anymore than anyone
else. The reality is they very seldom do any damage and usually do a lot of good. They keep your
cholesterol levels low by increasing your heart rate
to about 190 B.P.M. for the time it takes to stop
screaming, dancing and doing foolish things that
wake up neighbors or the dead.

CHAPTER

6

⁓⁓⁓

Going to a foreign country is something every person should do. The experience will forever change your perspective on the small things in life. Things like hot water, flushing toilets, carpeted floors. Things like clean water, electric lights, stop lights and cross walks. All these things are so taken for granted in the U.S.A. They are part and parcel of living here, yet the majority of the world know very little of these things.

When you go to places where these luxuries do not exist. You have a hard time complaining about anything, anywhere else you go and live. You would not believe the look I get from people when I break out in Praise and Worship, as my feet touch the Carpet, or the very loud groans of thanksgiving I express while enjoying the hot steamy shower. Even in the hot humid jungle, your thinking, I could really go for a hot shower, and it would help get the mildew out of my hair.

Another real shocker to the ignorant "Gringo" is how many people like warm Soda pop. All of the people that we were introduced to, were very friendly and either would offer a cup of nice hot coffee"Tinto", in little tiny cups that seem like they belong to a little kids play set. "Tinto" was the alternative to a soda. The question is always asked, cold or room temperature. Room temp is the popular answer, because most people have no refrigeration. It was hard not to gag at the thought of a warm soda but I was already sweating profusely, so Tinto was not a good option. What is not to like about a warm Coca- Cola, and you guessed it, it is one of those words that is easy to say in Spanish. Coca-Cola por favor!

There are many new palatable delights to experience and most of the time things are good.

You get a few that ruin your day or a couple of days, as you run to the bathroom, but you also get some that are phenomenal. One of the delights that I experienced was Crema de Coco. This drink was the best thing I ever tasted. I still to this day have not found anywhere that has replicated it. It was an icy drink made from Milk, sugar, coconut, ice and I don't know what else. It was so sweet, smooth, and had little chunks of soft coconut meat, not the shredded coconut I had eaten in pies during desert. I think it offsets the first bite of Blood sausage, that lingers in my memory as the total opposite of delight. I cannot begin to express the effects of the sausage, but it was a rough few days afterward.

Hunger is the best teacher of the tongue and unfortunately you can learn to like anything if you get hungry enough. Believe me, I got hungry enough and I can tell you most things are palatable. Some you hope to never repeat but….don't kid yourself, you can eat a lot of things you never dreamed of, and learn to like them.

One of the things I learned to eat had a funny name, it was called San Cocho. It was a stew, or thick soup that has many different ingredients, one which included chunks of green plantains. It took a lot of hunger to train my tongue but thru the years it was accomplished and now with great relish I enjoy. You can throw in a few pieces of meat or chicken and even make it better. Of course it is always served steaming hot, and will help you break a sweat if for some reason you haven't started yet. I think the hardest part of jungle missionary life was having San Cocho for breakfast. Any soup for breakfast, was tough to deal with, I was used to Wheaties, Coco puffs, or Oatmeal. None of that would be available or on the menu.

I ate many strange things in the years I was on the Caqueta. I must clarify that most Colombians do not eat what we Americans would chow down on as residents of the Mission.

My wonderful wife, who I encountered on the Caqueta, to this day still thinks I'm kind of dopey for having eaten some of the things we tried. Her opinion is, better to starve. She's probably right. She told me her father would throw the pots and pans away if he knew that some of the critters we cooked, had been used. He was the toughest, scariest guy I knew. Of course most future Father-in-laws are, aren't they?

On the Okay side of the food and pantry list, we'll start with Piranha…taste like fish. Horse… taste like mmmm… meat. Jaguar…. meat again. Armadillo, not to bad but not to good. Caiman, the Colombian version of crocodile not to bad, but I never liked it. Snakes of different versions, not very good and was difficult on the hard core Christians.

Every one thought we were eating Satan. I gave it up after a few tries. Just the thought of eating a bite of the devil kind of takes the hunger pangs away. Wild pig is good, but God help you when you are doing the butchering, they are a very nasty smelling beast. Tapir is okay, Capibari is good if you like Cod liver oil, Just saying… some foods are medicinal. Guinea Pig and Pigeons for example, nothing wrong with those. The best of the best was a creature called the Boruga. It is a brown furry forest creature that looks a lot like a twenty five pound rodent. This delicacy was nocturnal and not easy to get. Stuffed with rice and other goodies, and baked in the mud oven, made it the best of the best

On the bad side, and it was more perception than flavor was monkey. When someone hands you a roasted monkey arm, or leg, you just can't get over the fact that it looks so human. God forbid you are given the chance to cut your own piece off the carcass and the head is still attached. I mean you got to be one tough cookie to be able to chow down, on something that looks so much like a relative.

My exiting excuse was to mumble something like, I just ate and could not possibly eat another bite, or can I wrap it up and take it home for the wife to enjoy.

Iguana was bad, especially after a few encounters with them popping out of outhouse holes, literally scaring the crap out of you. They must have figured it was a smorgasbord in there, with the plethora of choices.

Sloth was just too tough. You take an animal that is so slow moving that its hair is an actual living biological entity, and it eats bamboo, leaves, and woody things, and to expect to get anything tender enough to chew, your kidding yourself, just not edible.

On the downright nasty side, I have to go with Anteater. You can probably guess this one real easy. They taste just like ants smell. Very Bad, and Very bad indeed.

For you who live in a place with few to no ants, like Alaska, it is hard to describe. I will have a chapter later in the book on these creatures but trust me, the last thing you ever want to put in your mouth is anything that smells like Ants. Been there, done that, and you really don't want that T-shirt.

Last but not least was a small little herb that was served on most everything. Cilantro, you either love this at first taste or really despise it. I was on the despise side of the coin. It was like adding

33

a spoonful of soap to whatever you were eating. Usually a nice hot bowl of SanCocho, was in front of you, or if you were lucky, bean soup. Cilantro was unavoidable.

I was courting my wife at the time of my conversion, from Cilantro hater to Cilantro lover. I was sitting at the table in her home with all of the family, invited to dinner, about to partake of a wonderful meal of Bean soup dodging the gruff looks of her Dad and brothers, as the soup was brought out.

My wife is the best cook I know. She has been cooking since she was a child and if she touches it, it is good. My Grandkids come to our house and ask for Beans and Rice, and a take home dish too, thats how good her bean soup is.

I'm seated at the table, ready to eat, spoon in hand, salivation glands in full blown overdrive, my eyes roving from the Delicious looking Bean Soup, to the stern future father-in-law, multiple indignant future brother-in-laws, and a suspicious future Mother-in-law, and then back to my soup. This delightful creature, my future wife, who I furtively glance at, so as to not raise the level of protective ire to Def-Con One, walks calmly around the table in her demure, quiet and lovely manner, and oh,…

so gently, garnishes a spoonful of freshly chopped cilantro into each persons bowl of bean soup. Like the wise Princess she is, she starts with her honorable father, and then her mother and down to the brothers, and of course last but not least, the despicable Gringo who is trying to ingratiate his way into such an honorable family, and can't keep his eyes off the prize child.

I never even see it coming, no way to wave off the incoming onslaught of finely chopped cilantro, delectable herb of delights. I, slowly stir the soup, never taking my eyes off of the gliding royal smile she bedazzles me with. I smile back and spoon in a mouthful of the best bean soup on the planet, never to ever complain about Cilantro again. Conversion completed. Love will make a way, Love will make a way.

CHAPTER

7

T he day has come for me to fly out to the Caqueta river and to start life at our new destination, the mission station known as La Cocha. It took me some time to understand the difference between, San Cocho and La Cocha. The Spanish language is by far the easiest language to learn and read. It is spelled phonetically, and is a beautiful language. It is easy to read, very descriptive, a little tricky when it comes to things being female or male, and is probably doomed to being Political Incorrect in the future. Why, for example is an axe, Male, and a Table, Female. Some one could go to court over this.

Why anyone would name the Mission Farm after a Stew was beyond me. Once I got there and spent some time there, it was a good name, and totally appropriate. but alas the name La Cocha, actually meant a back water area, or a part of the river that no longer flowed. It just sounded like San Cocho, to the untrained ear of a new kid, that was always hungry, but had not learned to eat hot stew at anytime of the day.

La Cocha is approximately sixty miles as the bird flies from Florencia. It spreads out on the side of the Caqueta River about two thousand acres of swampy jungle. In the year of 1972 when I arrived in Colombia, once you lifted off from the Florencia Airport and headed out, there was nothing but jungle. You sat in the back seat of a plane that is the equivalent of a grasshopper in cornfield, a speck in the vastness of what lies below.

I would like to say it was beautiful, but it wasn't. It was terrifying and stressful, especially not knowing where I would be landing, hopefully alive and not cooked by the air I was trying to breath.

There had already been two plane crashes where all persons on board had perished. One plane had crashed on the airstrip we were heading for and one in the mountains at the headwaters of the Caqueta river.

We flew in a little Cessna four seater, which the Mission owned. I looked out the little windows breathing the humid liquified air, observing what was just unidentifiable green massiveness. Bravely holding onto my freshly sharpened machete and its fresh leather case, saying quite goodbyes to the Cinnamon twins, while my parents were gladly heaving sighs of relief.

They had no idea what waited for them at the end of the short flight and I have to hand it to them, they were pretty brave and just down right ignorant. Ignorance is Bliss, but there is a price to pay at the end of the rainbow. Forty years later the truth and fictional accounts could appear in book form. I'm surprised others that were part of this story didn't write some of their own tales. Oh yeah I just remembered its not very easy to do this. It is also kind of painful. Kind of like the airsickness I was trying to keep down as the grasshopper bounced over and thru heated jungle air turbulence.

An hour flight and all you ever knew of civilization is gone. One little time slot of sixty short minutes, and life as a carefree American teenager was flushed down a hole, a vortex, a time warping, mind bending, sensory overriding, tornado. In mind, in soul, in spirit, like Noah after the flood, like Dorothy of OZ, like Lord Greystone, or like Mowgli, emerging from the wolf pack. Not knowing whether I belonged to the Jungle I was swallowed by, or the civilization I had been taken from. I would never, never be the same again.

Fourteen years later, a different person would emerge from the Jungle, a completely different character would be thrust back into civilization, with just as much ignorance, violence, confusion, and quickness. My life in both directions, coming and going was like night and day, hot and cold, polar opposites and as such, very powerful in the push of opposite directions. I can say I am blessed to have survived the rip tide force of extremities. I would also like to leave this upheaval of the mind, in writing to all parents as a warning of the future.

Children experience things in a totally different way than adults . They will remember each detail in a very different way than you do. Take care not to believe that what you are doing is good for your children, for you do not see the experience through their eyes and souls and they do not understand and never will understand what you have wrought on their beings. If and only if, by Gods grace he brings good from the experiences, you can read the stories and sleep at night. If not you can tear your own soul to shreds of regret for having in ignorance, or self deceit brought others to the brink of what no man likes to name.

All stories never end with you. The children and the children's children, will bear the marks of the memories, good or bad. Accurate or false they will be passed on and on, molting and changing colors, temperatures and volume.

CHAPTER
8

~--~_-~_-

T he arrival at the airstrip in the jungle was actually uneventful, a short flight and a new different life began to unfold. A baptism of sorts as I recollect it.

I crossed over a final frontier as I hopped out of the little plane. It would be two and half years before I ever got out of the jungle, and I would be so very different, and never the same. I did not know it at the time but we had landed on an island that was owned by Don Chepe. I would eventually marry his daughter, and that is for a later chapter. The island was across the river from the mission station known as La Cocha.

I gulped in the first breath of Jungle air, thick, sticky in its hot languid taste, motionlessness and oppressive. I unloaded my suitcase, trusty machete, and precious guitar. I then followed the airplane pilot over to the first obstacle on our way to "La Cocha". The swamp, that was breached by a round bamboo bridge, awaited our valiant brave attempt at a kind of high wire act. If you have never walked a high wire, I would discourage you from trying the smooth, algae covered, round bamboo bridge. Especially if you are in a new pair of oversized rubber boots known as La Machas. La Machas eat your socks, every step you take is one little tug until they are curled down at the bottom of the toes. The boots of course are also as hot as a waffle iron, so by the end of the first hour of wear, the socks are more like sponges that have been soaked to the fullest degree. By the end of the day they have a smell that is ripe and full of promise to being in competition with the cheese factories of famous renown.

Native Colombians never wear socks, they know it is an act of futility and a waste of effort but I never could get out of the habit and torturous delight. I learned to wash and mend socks like a champ. Socks don't last long in Cheese factory conditions.

Meanwhile, and back to the bridge over the swamp, a new factor in challenge appears. The bridge moves as you step on it. The slick bamboo rolls and slides and is damp from the mucous like slime that encases it from the dew of the morning and the humidity of the day. I think I made it three or four feet before sliding off into the underlying muck. The muck is an orange colored watery mass full of long green and yellow canes with long leaves of Saw grass. Saw grass is mean stuff. It cuts the skin more like a scalpel than a saw. It should be renamed Scalpel grass. You eventually learn to ignore the heat and cover your body, to avoid the skinning action of the grass. Imagine a thousand paper cuts, up and down your arms, then rub the sweat in to keep the attention focused, the mind in constant alert, screaming at you to avoid this plant at all cost. The only problem is it is everywhere and never ceases to grow at amazing rates. I've seen it grow six inches in one night. That is the usual growth rate for lots of tropical plants.

The orange color in the murky mud comes from the iron in the soil. I had never seen orange swamps in the movies, so it was a surprise.

The muck is only knee deep which fills up the "La Machas" quickly and add about thirty pounds of weight to each foot. No big deal as I, very quickly slog through to the end of the morass, expecting

to be swallowed up in quick sand from so many
Tarzan movies I remembered. We get to the end of
the swamp, which leads back up to a muddy beach,
and I realize we have actually come to the rivers
edge. The mission "La Cocha" is on the other side.

It spreads out under white splotchy trees and
I see what appears to be shacks of different colors and sizes but mostly brown and grey, Leafed
Roofs, and red tar papered hovels, all on stilts
and high posts. The plainness and bland colors
are surprising after having left Florencia, so full
of color and vivid attractions. It exudes an air of
challenge and labor. It was hard to reconcile my
preconceived imaginations and the reality of the
obvious. Not one tree house or Leopard skin clad
person to be seen.

My sweat pours thru the clean clothes I had
so cherished while strolling thru the town we had
left that morning. I was muddy to the waist, and
marveled that the Pilot had walked the bridge and
was smiling all the while, but mercifully not men-
tioning how pitiful I looked.

We were met by a strange apparition of a
man who came in a wooden dugout canoe. He
was standing in the back of it paddling, smiling
and gesturing for us to get in. He was dressed in

clothing that was smeared in black stains, top to bottom. I stared and must have really been gawking, when the pilot said, Its okay, you will look like that soon too. I was not impressed and could only try to ignore the despair I felt.

It turned out that I would look like that in a few short months. The Black Smear is the result of harvesting bananas and plantains. The green plantains, which are the bigger of the Banana family, are the biggest part of our future diet. When you cut a stalk of bananas off of the plant, it oozes a sticky fluid that as it dries turns into a black stain. It is called "Mancha". You get this on your hands and clothes and only with extreme diligence does it come off. Most people get a set of clothing that they use just for this job. So now on top of being hot, and wet and sticky, you are oozy, hot, wet, sticky and turning black from the mancha.

The dugout canoe is only eighteen inches wide. I was wondering why the fellow was standing up and soon realized that it was to narrow to sit down in. Pilot man turned and tells me to stay where I am, like I really am going to go anywhere, and the Stained apparition will be back for you and your guitar. He paddles off to the other side, and as I wait he disappears into "La Cocha". I wait

45

my turn and was soon ferried over with the black stained apparition spitting words at me like a machine gun. He was probably telling me that if I caused him to fall in the water he would make sure that I was eaten by the piranhas or caimans, but his big smile eased my fears and I was soon on the other side and swallowed by "La Cocha".

CHAPTER

9

L a Cocha was and is a real place. Most novels take real places and weave stories around them, as I do with this novel. If I had access to all the hundreds of people who lived there I could write for fifty years. My chapter on it will be short because I only lived there a couple of months and had no clue what was happening around me. It was like landing on the moon with a swim suit. I was not prepared nor understood a thing.

I was bounced around and floated from one crazy experience to another. It would be better said, I slogged through the experiences because it is the jungle after all, and there were only muddy paths to follow.

Day One, and I'm introduced to the mens dormitory. I am given a bunk and told to report to the dining hall, when the bell rings. Supper of some kind was issued, rice and plantain soup. I couldn't keep it down and soon reverted to my bunk in the steamy mens dormitory. Day two, a bell is ringing, and it is still dark but everyone is moving out of the bunks and back to the chow hall as light creeps over the horizon. People begin to sing, while the food is served. Everyone around was smiling and singing, I wasn't. I understood nothing happening but was sure that all was good until I tasted the coffee and breakfast was served. Rice and Plantain soup again. Again? And this coffee is not right. It turns out, t he hot drink is boiled Molasses Water.

For breakfast? Where do you find a bowl of Rice Krispies? It takes a few years of practice to appreciate a bowl of soup for breakfast, but you eventually can. The Rice Krispies never appeared and were only later to be found in torturous Malarial fevered visions.

I was soon abandoned on the path outside the dorm and watched as all the guys hurried off with their machetes, to gather around the "Stone". I grabbed my machete, now in imitation mode, and to their great delight, followed. They each would take turns rubbing their machetes on the stone, I would learn later that they were sharpening them, and it was to be a much practiced routine throughout the day. I thought mine was sharp because of the earlier ministrations in town, but had much to learn about what is sharp and what isn't. It takes a few years of practice to appreciate that too.

A wonderful guy walked up to me, all smiles and muscles, and shook my hand. He was about six inches shorter than me but with a clenched tooth grin began to try out his English. It was halted and slow but he introduced himself. I will call him Stacio, for the legal purposes of this novel.

He was my introduction to Mighty Mouse and his merry men. I found out that he and all the companions at the farm were like SuperMan in Rags. They didn't look like much but were so, so strong and tough. The endurance of a Colombian Jungle farmer is only comparable to a U.S.A. Navy Seal. Never underestimate a little brown guy in raggedy clothes and LaMacha boots, Never.

Stacio took me that day and introduced me to my first real jungle encounter. Life was never the same, and Tarzan books never held up under the reality of the truth. If you love Tarzan don't read any further, for it will be a reveal of Fake news.

First let me explain there are various types of jungle. Real Old growth jungle, of which there is very little left, in the area where we lived. This is the type where trees are twenty feet in diameter, and full of vines and hardwoods. The second type is what comes after the virgin jungle is cut and burned and then grows back. Trees that grow thirty and forty foot in height, much softer and faster growing. It only takes seven years for that to happen. This stuff is called "Rastrojo" pronounced ra-stro-ho. This makes up the huge majority of the "jungle" that was present at the time of my arrival.

My first day in the "rastrojo" was never to be forgotten. I scurried along behind Stacio trying to keep up, in the muddy paths that he glided over while I plowed thru like an ox in a pit. The spot where all the "brethren", little brown guys all in the same Superman in Rag costumes and LaMacha boots were waiting. We stood at the side of what looked like an impenetrable wall of tangled nastiness, that was green and brown in color and held no light. Their machine gun linguistics pelted me with who knows what derogatory comments, but they were all laughing and I smiled, and laughed along, not knowing what was to come. How was I to know that they were talking about me, as I would talk about future Americans when they showed up. In a split second the air was alive with a furious on-slaught of swing machetes, pinging and slinging, chips of trees, big green things, little yellow things flying by my head, it was like a living cyclone, I had no idea as to my roll in the death dance of flying metal, and spanish chatter. In a matter of seconds they advanced into the depths of what I thought was green hell, and started to vanish. In my wildest imaginations I was sure they were possessed by the evil spirits that I had been warned about in many a heavy sermon during my childhood.

Stacio was quickly disappearing with the rest of the banshees but had the nicety of soul, to beckon me to follow him into the fray and hellish mess that was being left behind. I futilely struck at a few sticks and leaves with my cudgel of a ma-chete, and at a distance followed the melee. After a while I realized they were clearing the underside and smaller stuff out of the way, in what is called a "Socola".

Stacio showed me how to swing my machete and I learned one of my first spanish phrases. "Mas Bajito", meaning LOWER, cut it lower. Lower for a

51

six foot tall American is about eighteen inches off the ground. To five foot six Stacio, its flat ground scraping level. Stacio forgot all his English and all he repeated for the next eight hours was "Mas Bajito". I learned that phrase real quick. He muttered it, over and over, and then probably decided to say a few Christian cuss words that I didn't understand, like "Gringo Estupido". He always smiled though while speaking and I never forgot it or him. I followed him and whacked my way through the day.

After a few hours I began to notice a lot of pain in my hands. Every slash and stroke was like fire and acid being mixed in a fiendish concoction and being applied to my hands. I slowed even further and just kind of walked behind Stacio, trying to avoid being smacked by flying debris, while the banshee troupe, seemed to speed up, and get louder. The truth of the matter was they did, and it was now time to eat lunch and sharpen the machetes. I held out my hands to Stacio, telling him I was in a lot of pain, he proudly held my hands up to show all the banshees and with a big smile, gently laughed and all the others laughed with him. I had blisters on every finger, joint and possible hand surface. His closed tooth smile broke out in a war cry of Joy.. "Muy Bueno".. spanish phrase #two. Very Good. The rest of the day was a painful blur. I was too proud to cry, but on the inside I was a puddle of tears. Stacio seemed proud of me and did not abandon me, though I'm sure he would have loved to, seeings that I did not do much in the way of cutting down the mess in front of us. The whole reason we were out there was to mow down the stuff and then to come back later and cut down the bigger stuff and then to plant corn, rice and beans. I would learn that art much later in the game, but day one was a real downer on a Tarzan fan.

That evening Stacio took me over to his mother's house, for some help with my hands. She was the smallest, little wrinkled women I had ever met. She smiled the same big smile as Stacio and then took my hands, examined them and exclaimed "No Bueno"... and I felt a little betrayed by Stacio who had said "muy bueno". She took me into her little kitchen where a black hunk of something alien and evil looking hung over the fireplace on a hook. She was gentle and kind but proceeded to cut a piece off of the alien hunk, and then rub it onto my howling hands. The crazy little lady was as strong as Stacio. She held onto me while rubbing my hands with the evil looking black stuff, I danced a jig and screeched a lot. It turned out the black stuff was dried beef fat, and tallow, hung over the stove to cure it and preserve it. She worked it into my raw open wounds and then offered me a cup of coffee. It's hard to hold a cup of coffee with bloody raw hands. I really wanted to throw it at Stacio, but he was just to nice and kept repeating, Muy Bueno, Muy Bueno.

CHAPTER

10

~~~~~

My parents arrived, with my younger brother Patrick, after about a month. They had been told that there was no room at LaCocha and they were needed to head up a new mission farm, that was about five miles upriver. A Colombian family had offered their land and service to the mission and were asked to raise Pigs for the mission. My Parents were volunteered for this task also. I have no idea what they had in mind but I'm sure that their arrival and consequential responses would have been a great chapter too. Unfortunately it was never discussed. They had been told that they were to start a new farm and they had sent a little money and some roofing ahead for their home to be built. It was ready, and off we went to the Farm we never did name, but was called after the owner, Tarkitos Farm.

We packed our small trunks and belongings in a borrowed boat and we journeyed up river for two hours to our new home. When we arrived we were greeted by Tarkitos and his wife and seven little children. They lived in a bamboo and leaf house, which was a typical river home, serving as a granary, and all purpose building. They all slept in a little side room together, which was about the size of a small Volkswagon beetle. I'm not sure how they fit in, but to say the least it must have been cozy.

Our new jungle mansion stood about a hundred yards to the side of their house. A little twenty four foot square box on stilts. Bright yellow split bamboo walls and a bright red Tar paper roof. I'm not sure what Mom and Dad's thoughts were but I'm sure it was not the Mansion they expected, and it sure didn't meet Tarzan standards. We were told to sweep the floors often, to keep the critters, bugs and other crawling things to a minimum and it would make the bamboo slick and polished.

My Mom was definitely able to grab a broom and if it wasn't whacking me and my brother Pat, it was swooshing the floors and walls. We had a well polished house.

The box house had twelve foot tall walls. The fellow that built it was told that "Gringos are real tall". It was very obvious that he was a short guy but we had to give him and "A" for effort and a few extra pesos for all the extra bamboo he had to cut down to make the wall coverings.

This was home for the future, and I still wonder, how my parents didn't turn around that day and head back to the good ole U.S.A. homeland. Mom with a big Hallelujah hung a sheet down the middle and claimed her room on the right, and me and my brother Pats room on the left. I think my Dad was wondering if he was going to ever, ever have marital relations again, but as all good Missionary families go, nothing was ever said out loud, and I guess they got good at being really sneaky about it. Thank God for lots of Thunder and Lighting Night Storms. I never did hear any tomfoolery going on in the house. It might have been because me and my brother had to sleep together and we fought like cougars over every inch of the shared bed under the oven like mosquito net. It was a daily event to see who could sneak one inch of space out of the other guy. We usually were so tired from the days work that I think we passed out fast, and slept the sound sleep of novice jungle dwellers. I suppose Mom and Dad probably did too, so tomfoolery was a back burner issue for a while, or at least till the Monsoon season.

CHAPTER

11

I have to give credit to Tarkitos and his family, they put up with us for a long time and became our Colombian Foster parents. They were just common country people, poor, hard working and tenacious. They had been converts to christianity and somehow had become affiliated with, and to the La Cocha congregation. I don't know how they came to the faith, but thankfully they cared for us in our ignorance and complete inability to care for ourselves. I always loved them and missed them, just for the fact that they didn't abandon us.

They shared what little they had and we learned how to survive on next to nothing. We always ate lunch together and after six months ended up eating all three meals with them. We ran out of money and supplies and had no idea how to eat what was grown and available on the farm. The only thing available was Plantains, Yucca, corn, rice, and any creature that was not able to escape our attention and fleet feet.

Hunger was a pervasive lifestyle and a continuous companion. A word of warning for any of you serious about living off the land or being a survivalist, it is not easy, fun nor a thing to trifle with. Be grateful for the advancements society and science have made. Only an idiot abandons the gifts that God has endowed us with in the 20th century. Hunger is a nasty way to die, and just because you are starving you will not get one inch closer to God. If that were true I'd be sitting next to the throne of the almighty himself, maybe just his footstool, but I'd be close.

One day Tarkitos wife, Tina, had a surprise for us. She was going to make us some fry bread. Oh happy day! We had not seen bread for a long time, nor had we eaten anything fried. There was an untold part of the story that would unfold thru the night but it was still a happy day.

We were so excited at the news that we all jogged out to work in the banana patch with glee as the lovely smell of hot grease and yeasty dough wafted about the fields. Tina's little stove consisted of two cement bricks spread out on a mud packed table with old machete blades crossing it from side to side. She would place the one or two cooking pots she owned, and with this simple set up, make a meal. Firewood was put thru the sides and the fire stoked up good to get the lard smoking hot. You could see her from the fields in her little kitchen on stilts, a couple of her babies crawling around her feet. The leaf roof was leaking smoke from the hot stove and good smells. On the back of the kitchen was an open window where a bamboo shelf stuck out over a big black puddle full of muck and murky drain water from washing dishes, babies and any thing else that needed cleansed.

The farm pigs loved the watery, mud pool underneath, as it held goodies from the dishwashing and suds. The cool mud pool was a great escape from the myriads of flies, bugs, gnats, and other winged creatures looking for fresh blood. The hogs would sink into the goo after snorting and bubbling through it for leftovers, and laying there with snouts and eyes only above the surface, completely content to smell the hot lard and bread dough rising. When she finally gave the lunch time

Yoooohooo call for us to come in, we all trundled to the feast that had tantalized us all morning long.

We had the usual hot San Cocho soup lunch, some boiled ripe plantains and then the wonderful hunks of Fried Bread, which had also been sprinkled with some white sugar that had appeared as miraculously as the bread itself. That first bite was oh! so wonderful, oh! so soft and doughy, the sugar melting on the back of the tongue, and then …..a subtle flavor I did not recognize. It was just there, kind of like in the back of your nostrils, slightly off, kind of like the smell you remember when you used to go to Grandpa's garage, where the old car sat, or when you bicycled thru the gas station to get air in your tires or to get a soda pop. I couldn't place the smell, but it was definitely triggering some strange memories for being in the middle of a bread eating festival.

It even got better because Tina came out with second helpings. Oh man, it was a great day, we were going to eat till we were full, an event that rarely happened. We all sat around with that wrinkled nose look but gobbling the goodies down and laughing at our good eats that day.

We soon were done and shooed out the door, back to the fields and off to work. It was hot as hot can be on a sunny jungle day, and we all soon began to feel a little woozy, and then to make things worse, I began to burp, over and over, and that strange smell would reappear, and seemed to get worse with each burp. As I looked around, all the rest of the guys with us were kind of in the same haze and burpey mode too. Finally someone said, I'm feeling like I swallowed a gallon of kerosene. At once I placed the smell with a memory, but was still confused as to the where, when and why. We made it thru the hot afternoon feeling worse as time went by. Finally we called it quits and retreated to the river to swim and cool off. By night fall, we were all in a bad way. The whole group of us guys smelled like a petroleum refractory belching clouds of noxious fumes. It was a rough night to say the least, thankfully there were no lightning strikes nor matches struck. It could have been disastrous.

At breakfast time we all gathered and shared our stories of misery and wondered how we didn't all die. Momma Tina, finally approached the table and with a repentative attitude declared she had a confession to make. As she watched her husband suffer thru the night she knew she had to let us know the reason for our gaseous plights.

She then elaborated how a couple of days before she had been taking care of the baby and had

knocked over the kerosene lamp and had not realized it. It had drained down into her little kitchen
cabinet where she had been storing the flour and
did not realize until later why she had not had to
clean up any mess. Nor did she know how much
had spilt.

The bag of flour had been soaking up the kerosene and she knew that flour was so precious she
couldn't throw it out and decided that if she fried it
up as bread, the kerosene would evaporate and we
would not even taste it.

Every time I hear the song "This little light
of mine, I'm going to let it shine", I get the urge to
light a match and burp.

CHAPTER

12

I become a veterinarian by proxy, in this chapter, not by choice but by necessity. When you become involved in animal husbandry, also known as a pig raisin', hog farming or in techno-lingo, Pork Production Manager, it still translates to Caqueta Spanish as "Chonchero". You don't need to be fancy about it, its an ugly, dirty job but someone had to do it and I was delegated by Mom to the position.

My clothes, and skin were always dirty looking, from the plantain ooze that turned black as it dries. That was the main food for our pigs, or "chonchos" as the colloquial term is used. Our chonchos were not the beautiful two hundred and fifty pound pink beauties you see in the Almanac, or at the State Fair. The Jungle version is usually a hundred pound, stiff black wiry haired, elongated, long nosed, elephant eared, wrinkled version of the same, if you have a wild imagination. The river nickname for the hogs was "Serrucho". A "Saw", long and sharp toothed, mean and lean. They also were usually a couple years old to get to that one hundred pound size, maybe even five or ten.

I learned later in the process, after doing some real book learning, that once the heat index gets over a certain temperature, animals go into stress mode and do not grow. Just like humans they just make it day to day and try to survive. My pigs had about 20 minutes a day that they were not in stress mode. Like from 2:00 a.m. to 2:20 a.m. on a good day. It really was a losing battle, but we sure tried to overcome the odds, and it was a real effort. I named and cared for a few of the more fortunate critters I had, with a leaf covered cement pen we built. We figured to give them extra attention, and possibly get them over the hundred pound hump.

It was hard to call them Wilber or Charlotte, due to their deformities and sheer meanness, but we gave it a try.

To work with them you had to be like an action movie star hero for Jurassic Park. The behavior of a two year old, stressed out, penned up, angry, hungry choncho was akin to a Raptor on steroids. They could shriek at a high pitched ear shattering decimal level that would make an audiophile proud to endure, then charge up to whatever barrier that was between you and it, snout in the air, teeth and fangs showing, blasting rancid breath, and slavering drool. They created and gave definition to Alien slime before it was invented. It was a real freak show for a city boy who's only thought was, "is this really where bacon comes from".?

As I approached Pen #1 where a nightmarish version of Wilber lived, I noticed he had a hole in his shoulder the size of a silver dollar. The hole in the shoulder was about three inches deep, open and oozing. As I observed the nasty site, I noticed another addition to the nightmare, it was full of wiggly maggots.

I decided at that moment I must retreat and loose a little of my hot stew lunch, even though I hated to loose the nutrition I desperately needed to retain. It was not a choice I could make. It was a loosing battle, as the smell of rot and other nasty things that accompany putrid flesh overcame my senses.

To my rescue appeared our Senior Veterinarian, the seven year old son of Tarkitos, "Fredo".

Fredo had been doing all the interpreting for us with the inane ability to baby talk to us with sign language and simple one word expressions. As his parents would jabber away in full phrased conversations about how useless American fools were, and why in the world we thought we should be in this part of the world, Fredo would boil it down to one or two words, Like STOP, WATCH ME! CAREFUL!

The Little guy who was actually a seven yr. old super hero in disguise, would jump in the pen, grab a rope, make a slipknot noose, snag the upper jaw of the screaming demon possessed apparition crossover of a Pig/Raptor, and drag it over for me to hold onto. As I held onto the rope in a tug of war with the possessed animal, who's sound level upped another 30 decibels right in my face, little Fredo grabbed a big chicken feather and a bottle of some nasty smelling, vile, black liquid and started digging in the hole on the creatures shoulder. Out popped maggot after maggot. Fredo giggled in delight as I lost the rest of my hot soup lunch. Of course that went pretty much unnoticed as the screaming and wrestling match continued on. After ten minutes of this frantic medical procedure, Fredo declared Victory and showed me the result. A hole big enough to put your fist in, and what looked like an irreparable injury. He then took a little more of the black Liquid, sloshed it around the wound and giggled as the creature bellowed and bucked, declaring with glee 'Muy Bueno". My pale grey face was kind of red from the shame of loosing lunch in the presence of a seven yr. old, the new example of Veterinarian's class 101, career teacher.

Next up was choncho #2 with one of its ears three times the size of the other ear. He walked around with it dragging on the ground looking like a One sided Dumbo. About this time Papa Tarkitos showed up and declared in rapid fire lingo which I of course did not understand, to lasso up patient #2. We or I should say Fredo, was quick to move and understand. He snatched the hog up by his snout, while the decibel level increased to 150, then handed me the grimy rope, still oozing from the last operation and motioned to hold on. Tarkitos slid his machete out of the fancy leather case he wore, and performed a quick surgical procedure. It would have made his medical predecessors proud, no hesitation as he sliced the pigs ear clean off.

Just like that, my perception of the veterinarian occupation turned into an abject fear of ever having to be part of the process. Little did I know what was to be in the future with me and Veterinarians.

Well…. back to the ear, as it was handed to me, like a deflated football, heavy and oozing blood. I wasn't sure what I was supposed to do, and passing out in a pig pen full of screaming Raptor/hog crossbreeds didn't seem wise, so I jumped the fencing and headed for the River, and tossed the ear into the river. Tarkitos and Fredo were giggling and rattling on in español, seemingly proud of the successful surgery. They grabbed a bag of salt, poured a bunch into my hand and motioned for me to apply it to the bucking mad screeching patients ear stump. Nothing like sticking a handful of salt on a sawed off ear to get the blood to stop flowing. I applied the Salty Balm, and beat a hasty retreat covered in slobber, filth and blood, and by the next day Old Porky was just fine, and fighting at the food trough just like the operation had been a hangnail removal. A few months later we had pork head stew, minus one ear, thankfully.

For those of you who have never had pork head stew, let me clue you in on a trick. First, don't look closely at what floats to the top. Second, don't dig deep to the bottom. Pork teeth don't float and hogs don't brush their teeth. Last but not least, pork taste like pork no matter what part of the hog it comes from. From snout to tail, when boiled it all tastes the same. It's not too bad, especially if you haven't had any protein to eat in a year or two. I still ask for seconds, when the bacon is passed around. I do prefer not to stir my pork stew.

CHAPTER

13

～—～＿～

66 "T he terror from above", is usually a term held for God, Angels, Fighter Planes, Lightening, or Thunder bolts. I use it for the small but effective tool God used to drive the Canaanites out of Biblical territories given to the Israelites during the conquest of the promised land.

Hornets, Wasps, Bees and flying insects that sting so bad you end up with P.T.S.D. for life, THESE are the true "Terror from Above", and the discussion of this chapter. I don't consider myself to be the most pain tolerant person around but I think the worst creatures in the Universe is the WASP. I'm not sure of the clear distinction between these horrid creatures but they all fit in the spanish category of "avispas", a word we quickly learned to avoid, dread, watch for and to fear.

I had been stung by a honey bee or two as a kid but the creatures that inhabit the jungle are not to be compared. I have seen a few horrid YouTube shots of huge wasp nests down in the south of the U.S.A. but in the jungle it was a nightmare unleashed. Most people fear spiders, cockroaches, big beetles, ants, which I also hate, but the "avispas" became the dread of my life on a daily basis. It seemed that no matter where you went, or what you did you were going to encounter these creatures and suffer immensely, every time.

My first encounter was actually with my younger Brother Patrick. We were taken to a bamboo patch a few days after having arrived at our new home. We had no clue how to cut down Bamboo, which is an art form of its own. We followed Fredo, our seven year old super hero in disguise, as he led us into the thick of it, and we slashed our way into a bamboo grove and knocked a few bamboo down.

When you are a novice in the jungle everything is hazy, either from the unrecognizable vegetation, and its abundance, or the humidity which is dripping off of you, and every plant around you. The little picture gets out of focus as you survey the green surroundings in layer upon layer of depth. Every Bamboo stalk is covered in long strips of thorns, inches long and tipped with scilia that when struck or scraped on your skin, itches and burns. You are concentrating on not stepping on these, which literally are everywhere. If you step on them they will go right thru your "La Macha" boots like butter, break off in your foot, get infected and cause misery for years, not a fiction, but fact! I had it happen to me.

To top it off, I am wondering when the tarantulas I was told live in the bamboo, would start raining down on me like missiles from the end of the world movies I had seen on Science Fiction Theatre. It was easy to miss the little yellow specks flying thru the air. The specks seemed to be getting denser as I hacked away at a stubborn limb of thorns hanging off the green bamboo I was intent on hacking thru without much success.

My brother Pat, was close by and started yelling at me, as did Fredo. Pat with his mouth wide open, soon was running and screaming, and I not wanting be be left behind also took hot retreat. I realized that the haze was moving frantically around me like a yellow tornado. Fredo was screaming "Avispas". Pat was screaming "Avispas". I was just screaming. You cannot outrun a Wasp, but distance helps.. so about a mile out I finally stopped to catch my breath, while Pat who was ahead of me stopped to spit and sputter and gag, tears in his eyes, his nose running and tongue lolling. He was gagging and in obvious distress. Fredo was right behind us with our hats and machetes and whatever we had flayed off in the retreat. Pat finally got out the few words he could, telling us he had a handful of the Wasp fly into his open mouth and sting him inside his mouth. It was a pitiful site as he swirled a bit of lukewarm sugar water in his mouth to assuage the terrible effects of the poison injected. Finally after a bit, we all had to laugh as Fredo, reenacted our hasty retreat with tears of glee. The Colombians had found a new entertainment as we were intro-duced to the insect world. We found out that about every ten feet in the brush, you will encounter a wasp nest. If you learn to look, you will see them first. If you don't then you get a fast injection of "move it". Then the Colombians would get a new comedy episode of "Crazy Gringos", and the Latin Chicken dance.

All wasps are not created equal, and that is a mere understatement. Some are not as painful as others. Some are bad, some are terrible. Some will make you swell, some will make you bleed, some will make you sick. Some will target your face, some will target your eyes, some will target your ears, and sometimes the bullseye is your lips. God help you, if you run into a combination. Horror movie makeup can't compete with the grotesqueness of a full onslaught.

The size of the Demon horde nest is also relevant. Some nest you can swat with the broad side of your machete and smash it to smithereens, and run. Other nests are so big that only fire and bravado of immense proportions can be the answer. Some are up too high in the trees to even see, but when in doubt, run, flail and gyrate to save your hide.

The size of the wasp itself is also of significance. Some are pretty small and irritating, like the little Sweat wasp which would land on your arms to lick the salt. They get tangled in your body hair, and though not an aggressive wasp, he would sting you only if you dared touch him while he crawled around on you licking and tickling you to death. They constantly had an opponent wasp who would land on the first-comer and would wrestle with them, to see who could drive you nuts fastest. While fighting amongst themselves, if you resisted the tingling tickle they would decide to sting you, just so you would swat the other guy.

The wasps got bigger as they got more aggressive. The largest wasps I ever encountered were big blue black ones about three inches long. They hunted for spiders in the ground and were usually alone. They are very hard to knock out of the air, no matter how fast you were with the blade, and believe me I became very fast.

There were wasp of every color, and multicolored. Big purple wasps, that we called Congas, were the winged version of Conga ants. If you were stung by one of these it would leave you dripping blood and feverish for a day. Black wasps with white wings would chase you forever. These were called buzzards, "chulos". You could hardly find the nest to destroy them they would attack from so far away.

One wasp was unique in that it was symbiotic. This wasp was black with yellow wings and they made nest in the trees where the black and yellow "Curillo" birds lived. The two creatures, bird and wasp, worked together. These black and yellow winged birds wove nests that hung like Christmas ornaments in the trees. If you came near their trees or their birds nests, they would go peck on the wasp nests and a flurry of vengeance would descend on you.

One Wasp that I really hated was called the "Carniseta". The "Meat-eater". It was about an inch long, pale white, or grey in color and apparently liked to eat dead stuff. If it stung you, you wished you were dead. They would make you swell up so bad. My poor brother Pat got stung on the lip by one. His lip was so swollen it split open like a squashed banana.

It was hard to see him from my eyes that were swollen shut from the inflicted stings, but I was too busy wishing I was dead, to make fun of him. We really hated those creatures.

One day an Indian fellow, joined our congregation. We thought he was the most amazing person we had ever met. He performed a feat of deliverance we thought should have killed him. We came across a nest of these Meat-Eaters and it was huge. It was three foot long and full of thousands of these creatures. They would flutter and jitter at the sound of our voices, much less the movement of any of the jungle around them. They would squirm over the nest they had built in a skin crawling design of warning with explicit signals of dire consequences if bothered in the slightest way. They were not happy with our clattering, hacking machetes and loss of jungle brush cover. The Indian, "Seraf" took his shirt off and then began to rub his armpits with his shirt. He then came over and asked us to let him rub his shirt on our arm pits. After a flurry of discarded shirts and bare armpits, we retreated to watch the amazingly brave man. He had the biggest smile and the whitest teeth and the blackest eyes I had seen on a person. It was all I would remember as I thought of what I would say at his funeral, as they dropped his wasp stung bloated body into the river or grave. He then took his shirt in his hands and turned his back to the nest and began to approach very slowly telling us to guide him as he would not turn to look at the nest. He raised the shirt over his head and stood right under the huge nest as it squirmed in anger and bristled with a huge flurry of whistling wings and pale pain inflicting madness. Seraf stood as still as a statue and it began to look like a snow storm around him. The wasps started a cyclonic action that filled the air with a buzz of anger and winged fury and enveloped him like snow in a tornado. The flurry swirled and swirled and lifted off into the sky, and he finally lifted his head as the buzz ended, and gently broke off the branches the nest had been woven into. Not one sting, not one welt, not one anything. It was the most frightening thing I had experienced to that day. He turned around and offered us all a close up look see, which I declined out of abject terror.

I had to also fight down the desire to kneel at his feet thinking I am in the presence of a god, or run for fear that he was in league with the devil. A good christian doesn't think these thoughts but boy... I was a believer that what he had just done was supernatural. He did a few other things like that which were uncanny and made me respect him. You wanted him with you but not too close, just in case he was in in league with the dark forces. He definitely was one of the most fearless people I ever met. So for all of you of faint hearts, be of Good courage. Do not call me for help, and always rub your own armpits, mine are probably not in good condition.

CHAPTER

14

I n every good book, there has to be a fishing story with a whopper of a lie involved. It just stands the test of time that none of what you read and only half of what you see is true. This novel will not be the first book to make light of that fact, and you will have to go to the jungle yourself to determine the veracity of the stories I will tell but I can guarantee you that you probably shouldn't be swimming in the water.

The Caqueta river is different every day, one day it seems sluggish, brown, smooth, and thick like chocolate milk. The next day it seems clear, quiet and lazy enough to float to the Amazon, without a care. The next day it is ugly, frothy with nasty white and brown foam, swift and dangerous.

On really bad days it is full of big "chambas" floating islands of driftwood and clumps of jungle torn loose as it roars itself into fury and angry waves of trash and broken trees and bamboo splinters. It was a terrifying factor in flood season, as it literally drowned the land and left no dry land anywhere, with heaps of ants and bugs clinging to anything that was attached to solid surfaces.

I thought of the Caqueta river as a female, as a "she persona" that was alive and had a spirit like quality. On a moonless night the river was so black you would get vertigo, and it seemed to swallow you like ink. On a full moon night it was picturesque in full blown glory so much that you could think of nothing more beautiful and serene. It is a black and white picture from a photo album of great value.

The one thing you did learn after years of living on her, in her, above and below her surface, was to respect her and be aware of the illusion of tranquility, for she was truly a mystical presence, dangerous to say the least, when in an ugly mood.

We Americans were pretty crazy and should have realized that when you see all the Colombians sitting on their little balsa wood platforms dipping water with a gourd or utensil of some sort to bathe, it would be a good idea to stay out of the water. The Natives very rarely would swim or jump in the river. We. Americanos of course introduced them to running and diving and swimming from one side of the river to the other. They rarely participated and we thought of them as kill joys, no fun at all. After a few years and a little wisdom, a few scares and scars, I kind of lost the joy myself. I suppose I ought to be glad I lived to tell the story.

The first catfish that I caught weighed a hundred pounds. Oh, you say that is not so bad, what could be the problem? Well..... They have big boney Horns on the sides of their bodies, by the gills that stick out up to twelve inches long. One buddy of mine who caught a small twenty five pound catfish, was unhooking it in the boat while it thrashed around and the horn went thru his ankle. The horn has small serrated edges all going the wrong direction. Like a fishhook, the serration is directional so as to not come out. When it does, by much effort, agony and pain, it shreds and rips vital tendons and blood vessels that spurt enormous amounts of blood. This is not a pretty sight. The biggest catfish I caught weighed two hundred and fifty pounds. My friend Tim and I had to sink the canoe we were in, to get the fish into it. We then bailed all the water out, to re-float the canoe, to get home with our trophy. I used the horns off this fish for a corn husking tool for years. The mouths on these fish are a foot wide, and full of small hooked edges. When you look down the throat of a big catfish you really do begin to believe the story of Jonah and the Whale and the joy of swimming kind of goes down a notch.

Tim is my best buddy, and is the other guy on the cover of the book with me. We were rowing up the river and I was in the back of the canoe, steering and swapping fish tales with him. We were under some "chipero" trees, that over hang the bank of the river, and the branches were full of little birds, that spooked and scattered as we passed underneath. We were in a small dugout canoe rowing against the current when a flock of these little birds flew out in front of us and suddenly a gigantic catfish flew out of the water and swallowed one the birds, crashing back into the water beside us, almost capsizing us. I wasn't sure if I wet my pants, but since they were soaked, I could use the story as a good excuse. I'm not sure what Tim's excuse was.

Piranhas are a nasty fish and just plain brutal. I have caught them in all sizes. The big blue ones that are like twelve inch frying pans. The little silver and red ones that move in schools by the hundreds. They are all hard to catch because they can bite through any fishing line and netting like wet papermache. If you really want to catch them you use your old guitar strings for steel leaders on your line. You might have a chance, maybe. Their teeth fit together in a perfect scissor action and they can cut thru anything. I have seen them bite metal fishhooks and break them. If your hand gets in the way, the chunk they take out is literally surgically removed in a perfect circular gulp. They swallow the chunk as it is removed so there is no going back and repairing the injury, and it is painful to say the least. A good friend of mine lost a good inch of flesh out of the palm of his hand, and a lot of sleepless nights followed, as his wound painfully healed. When they get caught in your throw nets you can hear them "bark". They make a sound like a small dog barking. If you hear that noise while retrieving your casting net, you do your best to flood the net so it opens and they can get out. If they don't get released you're going to spend the rest of the day mending a hole the size a dolphin could swim through. You learn to carry a small baton to smash their jaws, because with every flop of their body they are biting and ruining your day.

I left a fishing line out one night and when I went to retrieve it I couldn't get it out of the water. It was stuck, or I thought it was, until it began slowly moving. I eventually retrieved the line, hook and eighty pound sting ray. Wow, Sting Rays are some ugly creatures. I know that in Vietnam they have caught six hundred pound ones and I am sure that we probably had some that big but they just broke our lines and were not going to giving it up. The stinger on a Ray is very venomous and can really ruin a day at the beach. Their long tail will whip around and cut and stab you and break off the poisonous covered barb. It kind of puts a kink in playing beach volleyball in the water.

The annual run of "Bocachico" a type of carp, was a festival for the fishermen who, like me tirelessly pursued them. They would school up by the thousands and we would use our throw nets to catch them. We would smoke them, salt them, dry them, grind them, and eat as many as we could before they would turn green with mold from the humidity, and dampness that invaded every aspect of jungle living. I threw my net on a school of them that was so thick that they literally picked my net out of the water and escaped. It was like catching an elevator on the way up. The catfish would chase them, and they would explode like fireworks out of the water in a silver cascade that would shimmer and slide in the moonlight, shooting out of reach of the hungry maw and teeth, eager for the feast.

Another beauty of a fish was the "Denton" tooth fish, also known as Pariya. This fish had fangs up to three and four inches long. They have pocket cavities in the skull that let them pass through so they could open and close their mouths. One day I was retrieving a hook from the water and as I raised it out of the water with a bait fish still attached, one of these fifty pound furies leaped out and snatched it out of my hand. It happened so fast, I didn't even flinch. I was lucky it missed my hand and grabbed the bait. My brother Pat was bitten by a small one and it was quite the chore to pry the creatures mouth open far enough to extract his hand from the fangs that went clean through his hand, it was especially hard to accomplish while he was screaming and carrying on, for some reason. Darn things are like bulldogs, they just don't want to let go.

Then of course you have our favorite toy, the electric eel. The kids used to love catching these marvels of nature. A whole group of kids, usually ten to fifteen of them would all hold hands while someone would rub the side of the eel with a machete, and everyone with glee would jump and scream as the current passed thru the crowd and wickedly shocked them all. I dislike eels. One time my throw net got caught on some underwater debris and I dove in to loosen it and whoa!! I learned to be like Jesus and walk on water. I got shocked so hard I literally jumped out of the water to the surface and was on shore without one stroke or sputter. My glassy eyes refocused after a few minutes and when the muscle spasms slowed to a minor pulsation of 240 beats per minute I re-evaluated the value of my net. I left that net to sit for a while, and contemplated that flying kites on cloudy days might be a better option.

On the Monongeti creek where I lived for a while, I saw an electric eel that was longer than my seven meter dugout canoe. That's twenty one feet!!. I was sitting in a clear spot fishing and the water of the Monongeti is black and clear. When the sun hits it just right you can see deep into the water. This big thing swirled by me and I thought it was an Anaconda snake swimming below the surface of the water. I saw it go and go and go, then its head surfaced. It was an electric eel, blowing out the silt from it gills. I had been thinking it was a good day for a swim, and then decided maybe not.

Please pass the soap and get back on the raft, there's a good reason the natives don't swimming the river.

CHAPTER

15

The ability for the human body to endure pain, to either ignore it or push through the agony is a science. I cannot intellectually and scientifically pontificate on this subject, but experientially I can tell you a few stories that defy logic and now that I am an older, I wish I couldn't tell. This being a work of fiction of course allows for great augmentation and leeway. Exaggeration and flat out lying are for the sake of the readers, because who likes the boring truth?

My blistered hands was just a teaser of the realities of Jungle life, and the future that awaited my body and its abilities. As you lay in bed reading this novel, or sitting in the sun on the porch swing, let me introduce you to a few of the mind benders, and how the hell did I ever do that "moments".

I'm staring at a tree that we are splitting into fence posts. This tree is called "barabasco". It is used for fence posts or building foundations. It is a deep brown color, and smells of tobacco and oil and smoke. It feels cold like glass to the touch and its splinters are like shards of Ice, sharp and hard. It is also a tree that doesn't rot. It is so hard that when the ax strikes, it sends sparks, and small pieces of your ax flying. There are a couple of different types of this tree, one called "Aumado" another one called "Granadillo". The one thing both trees have in common is they are heavy as rock. Really, heavy and then of course they are usually covered in Ants. Everything in the jungle is covered in Ants. If it isn't covered in ants then its covered in something worse that you will regret touching.

Two friends of mine, Seraph the Indian and Nando the mighty, are facing each other swinging their five pound axes, trying to split this Aumado tree open. With each axe blow, face to face slowly sliding the length of the tree, they open the tree to expose the inside which contains more ants. With a few more blows and a cracking sound the tree splits open and the process is done over and over till a stack of posts is left, ready to move. I, as a newly arrived ignorant one, am expected to start carrying these heavy ant covered monstrosities to the river, where our boat is. These posts are twelve feet long, twelve inches in girth, and weigh about 150 pounds. We load them onto the boat, so we can take them home for fence building, and various other uses. Newly arrived ignorant humans, should not be confused with horses, which are smarter and know that these posts are just too darn heavy to fool around with. Since we have no horses, I am shown how I should be grabbing one of the ant covered behemoths, and putting it on my shoulder and trot off through the jungle. The path back to the river is more like an obstacle course through hell. I begin my first class in Pain Management 101.

This ant thing is really a bother, as they crawl up my hands, down my arms, onto my sweaty neck, and begin to dig their little pinchers into my sweet white virgin skin. Lucky for me, this ant nest is of a type that doesn't have stingers. These suckers just bite and hold on. Of course there is an even better group of ants on a different kind of tree that are so tiny you can't hardly see them. Their invisibility sneaks you into a carefree attitude until they release their urine as a poison. As they crawl on you it feels like battery acid, and you feel like you have been bathed in liquid fire.

I cannot decide which pain is worse, the ants digging in ferociously or the heavy, slicing weight of the tree itself digging into my shoulder. What I thought was my shoulder is now just a bundle of agonizing nerve endings. I stumble and trip over roots and vines that straggle across the path and slog through the mud and swamp holes. I can't decide if I should stop and change shoulders or try to swing it to the other shoulder with a rolling action that I saw a few of the little Colombian guys do, like a magic trick. I stop, and try the easy way by dropping the post, into the wet path, slopping a little mud on it and dislodging a few hundred ants who really get irritated at being shook up. I try as hard as I can to pick up this post and realize I can't get it up, much less onto my shoulder. I also don't have the initial help from the ax wielding professionals who straddled me with this burden originally. Oh joy! I see one of the guys coming my way, back from the river, and I ask for help. As he helps me lift, I decide to go for the left shoulder on this next leg of the journey. Now of course I have angry ants, and wet nasty jungle ooze, along with some slick mud to accompany the profuse amount of sweat I have bursting out of my ant punctured skin. Once the post is loaded back on my shoulder, I turn on the speed to a maddening trot.

The dismaying reality that my left shoulder hurts twice as bad as my right one did, starts to sink in. I sway, and grunt and pant, and then try the magic shoulder roll I saw the little Colombian guys do so effortlessly, and screech in pain as the log rolls over my spinal column and scrapes the tight pinched skin that is still being happily dug into by a myriad of angry horned ants. The shoulder pain on the right shoulder is just as bad as it was the first time, and now it seems that the log wants to dive forward instead of hanging backward. Because of my lack of balance, I fight to keep the post from driving me faster and faster through the obstacle course path from hell. I try to catch up with the weight that is pulling me in a demonic pace, and it just never is quite achieved. Oh, Glory I shout, as the river is in sight, and I think I'm going to make it, when my foot catches a root and Bam!, down I go, face first into the muck. The log is now pinning me into the ground, like a knife edge in a watermelon. I feel like my shoulder is splitting, and I wonder if I'm going to drown in the mud before I die of asphyxiation from the pressure exerted on my carotid artery. I squirm in agony, and push my back into the mud and am able to get my arm out from underneath the post. I right myself, into a prone position free from the pain, yet short of the goal. As I finally get to my feet, the little Colombian fiends, come sailing by with two of these posts stacked on their shoulders, while smiling and mouthing the words, "No Problema", I really didn't want to hear it, so I turned and wiped my tears and a few of the angry ants out of my hair.

A week later that path was a little wider but a whole lot muddier. I learned to never, never, NEVER put down what you had already picked up, and that the pain on one side would always be worse on the other.

There is pain, then there is bearable pain, then there is torturous pain, then there is mind numbing pain, then there is bad pain, then there is just… …..forget about it pain.

Can't we get a horse? Oh what I would have given for a horse!

CHAPTER

16

_—~_—

There are idioms and expressions that make no sense to a person, unless they experience what created them, and the circumstances that they develop in. The Caqueta version of that is a "conejera".

Conejera should translate into a word suggesting an invasion of rabbits, but is actually the word used by the Caquetanians for a flood.

A legitimate Caquetanian is someone born on the shores of the Jungle River Caqueta, which flows thru the Department of Caqueta, located in the lower corner of Colombia, spelled with "O's" and no "U"s. The Caqueta river is a headwater of the Amazon river. Everyone knows about or has heard of the Amazon but has no idea of how much water they are talking about. The Caqueta river flows down from the mountains, and about a days distance away in a nice canoe with an outboard motor, you come to the little town of Curillo. On a not so nice day it could take you a week, give or take which way the wind is blowing and the amount of water falling from the sky. My future Father-in-law founded the little town and used to travel up to the town of Villagarzon, where my future bride was to be was born. With the native Indians rowing at full bore it was at least a week long trip. You had to be willing to swill down the home made liquor you were offered or you would get nothing to eat. The liquor was produced by masticating Yucca roots and spitting the goop into a gourd and letting it ferment for a week or two. That sounds like a trip everyone would want to make. It gives a new meaning to Free drinks, and all you can eat river cruising. Drink up or starve, almost sounds like a South Beach Keto diet on steroids. All the better for the rowers as the load got lighter while they headed up river and you procrastinate on the free drinks. Praying that the river doesn't flood making the trip longer and harder, was also a regular ritual.

As a teenage city slicker, I had never experienced a flood. I had never seen much of anything more than an overflowing soda cup at the Seven-Eleven store. The word "FLOOD" is a word for sermons and fiery preachers. When the soft rain started in February and kept falling, day after day, the new word we kept hearing was "la Conejera". It was spoken with a look of dread, and unusual activities like grabbing chickens and throwing them up in the rafters of the house.

On day three of the soft rain, I woke up to the miserable wet damp smell of mildewed clothes that due to the 110% humidity, had not dried thru the night. They had been soaked all of the previous days while out whacking at the jungle growth that never stopped. A sound that I could not place was also in the air. I stepped out to our balcony perch that faced the Caqueta river and saw that our house had been moved to the middle of the river. I could see what appeared to be a sea of white foam, on nasty blobs of chocolate Milk froth, mixed with dirt and clusters of trees and stuff being swept by the house in a rush of, milky, plum grey fluid.

There was no dry land to be seen. All of the surrounding houses were like us, in the middle of the river. HOLY! MOLY!, My head exploded, as I realized what must have gone thru the mind of Noah, as he woke up on that day of the great flood.

"Dang I'm glad I built the boat". My problem was I had no boat, and thankfully, no animals other than our parakeet.

I stood and watched, with my Mom and step-dad who were pretty pale from the realization of possible death and that the end of the world might be here. Were it not for the the jovial folks living next door who were busy cooking breakfast on their porch, and acting as if the world was not ending, we might have lost it.

Tina, and Tarkitos and their children were sitting up on their porch, waving and laughing and probably saying things that went along the lines of "those crazy gringos are going to drown, and die, or go home, if they live thru the next few days". We of course laughed back and waved and hoped they would not let us die or drown and starve on our own porch.

After a short while, Tarkitos who had known what was coming and had been moving all the canoes and boats thru the night, paddled over and tried to explain that we would be okay and we would probably not die. There was work to do so, we donned our wet clothes and waded out into the murky waters to help round up the animals and begin to salvage what we could.

We went out to the pig pens and began to move all the hogs, which were up to their snouts in the rushing water but had not washed away, being locked in the pig pens. We put them into the one larger canoe we had, and what a fight. You would think the animals would know, we just wanted to save them. Ours were not blessed like Noahs pigs, content to enter the ark of salvation and crossed off as saved from eternal extinction. Nothing is as challenging as lifting up a hundred pounds of bristled wet, snapping and snarling mad pig, dumping them into a canoe with another dozen pigs, all drowning, and mad about the total loss of porcine peace of mind. The ruckus and chaos, foaming mouths, pig poop, and murky water that was everywhere had no effect other than giving the "End of the World" doctrine another Depth of Meaning.

When we finished that rescue effort we began to search for our cattle. We had a small hill on the farm where the water was only knee deep. As we found them we roped and slogged the animals up to that higher ground, where they, unlike their porcine fellows, they gladly stood quietly ruminating and watching the world float by.

We went to bed that first night of the flood and I wondered if we would drown in the night, as the rising water splashed thru the cracks in our floor.

We had no where to go and no way to leave the house. It had become our personal island. No one would come for us, or even know we were gone. The water roared by the trees that had not been uprooted by the torrent. Big islands of uprooted floating bamboo, trees and detritus smashed and boomed its way down the river. The sucking sound of water swirling around the house posts, creating a small whirlpool at the back end of our porch was like a clock that needed rewinding. The occasional crash of debris hitting other objects make sounds to remind you that time was passing, the world was passing, and that you were a finite, small piece of nothing compared to the vast deluge that grew in its power. The little wobbly flame of our kerosene lamp we had placed on the table seemed the only thing that kept the end of the world and darkness from swallowing us. I dreaded the moment Mom would extinguish it, fearing that it would be the last thing I would ever see. It was a long night.

The amazing thing about a flood through the Jungle is the insects. Millions of spiders, ants, roaches, millipedes, centipedes, bugs and beetles of all kinds, end up on the fences and trees, or anything protruding out of the water. It begins to create a coating of living creatures, They sit still, immobilized by instinct to survive, not bothering to push, pull or contend with each other. What normally would have been a fight to the death, with stinging and swarming, biting and stabbing, and all out war of the species, just stops. They cling to whatever they can, be it wood, wire, or object and become still. Their inertia to move stops and they cling to each other knowing that movement will only worsen their predicament. I could stick my finger into the mass of insects and not one would bite, they just squeezed over and tightened onto the next bug. Nasty to behold, but incredible to contemplate.

As the water rose higher the smaller dislodged rodents and animals would swim by forced to look for dry land. That soon led us to chasing them down and getting ready for a dinner feast. It was an unfair deal, and we weren't very much like Noah. We had not prepared an Ark, and were not worried about repopulating the earth with unnamed jungle critters.

We captured a nice number of unfortunate critters and had a couple of good hearty meals. Of course the few rabbits that we encountered were down on their luck too. Lucky rabbits feet are overrated. Rabbits are not very good swimmers, or climbers, thus their population is scant and we barbarians took advantage of their plight. That being said, they sort of had their revenge on us, as we took advantage of them. We soon developed incredible jungle rot in indescribable places because of being wet for days on end.

When you are wet for days, your skin goes beyond the prune stage, and begins to take on an Applesauce texture. You don't want to touch yourself for fear something might fall off. Blue Jeans Levi's are the worst thing in the known world to wear in these conditions. Its guaranteed that the loss of cellular structure will be devastating. God help you, if you are in Commando Mode, for there will be no amount of Gold Bond talcum powder, vaseline, or other concoctions, that will repair the damage. There is a reason that fish wear no clothes. All those nudie pictures in National Geographic of the Native peoples are pictures of really smart people. Wet skin and clothing are not a match made in heaven, and after a few days of soggy Jeans you quickly wise up. By the end of the week I so wanted to be a heathen and free myself from the torment of wet frayed Levi's.

The water rose for three days, then stayed for three days and then took three days to subside. The whole time there was no sunshine to dry out our wet clothes. Murky, humid, sweaty heat, soon took its effect. The cattle soon began to loose their skin from the belly down. The grass and land that was beginning to appear, was covered in three inches of stinky mud. The stink, the ooze, the heat, the bugs now released from captive inactivity, and the huge puddles of rotten vegetation and masses of dead creatures were truly a feast for the organisms that turn decay into a new cycle of survival. Very few rabbits survived to partake in the regeneration.

The released pigs thought they had arrived in heaven. True to form they buried theirselves up to their snouts in the succulent muck. Pigs are incredible creatures, truly capable of making a feast out of famine. It's hard to believe hogs taste so good, after the nastiness they ingest, and love to inhabit. The gusto they display as they snort and snout thru the green and purple fetid pools of decay, either make you want to clap with applause or turn and hurl. It's all a matter of perception, and mine was visions of pork chops and stuffed baked pig "lechona". Chow down, baby, Chow down!!!!

It took months to get things back to normal, we treated the cattle daily for hoof and mouth Disease. All our Plantain orchards died, all of our Yucca rotted. All our corn was destroyed. Our rice crop was the only thing that was not effected. We ate a lot of rice that year.

Tina finally threw the chickens out of the rafters, back out into the yard. I was kind of getting used to the clucking and it made finding the eggs a little harder. Rabbits? well I never saw them again either. And that is how the "conejera" came every year.

CHAPTER
17

_ - ~ _ ~

Insects shall inherit the earth. The Bible says maybe the righteous will too, but its hard to be righteous. Bugs on the other hand have it made. Growing up in a city of Mid-West America, like Denver, you have the wonder of an occasional grasshopper who got lost and made the wrong turn out of Kansas, or an occasional rolly, polly bug kicked out from under a rock. The few ants I found, were objects of delightful hours with Grandmas magnifying glass, and not to be feared. I remember a few tomatoes worms and butterflies and of course the lightening bugs from vacation in Arkansas. But nothing and I mean NOTHING prepares you for the surprise nature has in store for those who are ignorant enough to stumble into Virgin jungle with stupidity as your guide.

I believe that God made everything but boy, oh, boy, he really set us up for a lesson in humility when he made Bugs. Insects are inventions from hell, and were brought by Lucifer when he crawled out of the Pit. Okay I know that doesn't fit the biblical theology but WHAT!!?? was God thinking when he created this part of creation? Hell is an awful place as it is described in many a Pentecostal Sermon which I observed in my youth, but let me tell you, eternal flames are no match for the torment to be unleashed upon the Earth when mankind blows itself up and Insects reclaim their rightful place as inheritors. After a few years in the Jungle, just when you think you've experienced every torment an insect can inflict, WHAM! you find another bug you've never seen, smelled or been stung, bitten, stabbed, poisoned by. What the heck can be worse than the poisonous burn of an almost Invisible Ant that urinates toxic. The acid that burns like hell fire and you can't even find the source its origin. The "Mahenia" also know as a piss ant is almost microscopic. You can't see it unless you really know what to look for. It is so tiny and the same color as your sunburnt, heat fevered skin, that it is unnoticed until the burn starts. It crawls down your bare neck or arms, sometimes your face, spraying its toxic poison, and you feel as if you are in Hell, burning in torment and you haven't seen your first Demon. You don't even see your adversary as you whack your way thru the jungle. They drop out of the trees onto you, crawling into the comforts of cotton, linen and polyester which was still in style at the time. Being burnt alive is not a joke, just an everyday experience for the foolish jungle dwelling invaders, who have given up Levis for polyester.

The amount of ants in the jungle is beyond fathoming. They come in all sizes, up to one inch long. They stink of garlic, licorice, cayenne, pepper, mud, mold, and other smells that have no description in language. They come in all colors, black, brown, purple, red, orange, yellow, and multicolored. They live in all kinds of odd places and above all, in the trees. All the Tarzan movies you ever see after living in the jungle are such a disappointment. The LAST place on earth you are going to live, is in a big tree. Trees are the worst and deadliest places to be. They are full of territorial, mean, poisonous, aggressive bugs. Bad things happen to people who live in or near, or below big trees, that should be full of tree houses. Oh! the disappointment when I saw my first huge tree with its possibilities of tree house construction, and swinging vine lessons. Upon approaching the colossal wonder I found it covered in one inch long Bullet Ants! The sound of an angry, bullet ant nest will make every hair on your body stand up in Fear and Trembling. One sting from this demonic creation will make your Traumatic Stress Syndrome permanent. No amount of professional counseling will ever get you over it.

Of course we haven't even got to the spiders, which the variety and color would make a circus on psychedelic meds compete in full out frenzy. Their arachnid size and variation can fill volumes. Hairy or Slick, compact or spread out, they inhabit trees, hiding in all kinds of unseen places, usually found by screams, shrieks and usually a few curses too. My last encounter with one of the delights was a few years ago while putting on my pants. To the tearful delight to my wife, and cousins and anyone within a mega decibels distance, the yelling was of record setting proportions.

As I donned my britches one bright jungle morning, during my last visit to the relatives home, the big hairy brute scampered out of the inside seams just as I got them knee high. I'm sure the creature was just as surprised as I, that my screaming, jumping and dreadful yells didn't produce the cockroaches he was looking for down in the wrinkles of my pants. I think I tore an ACL and a Hamstring, but I did avoid being bit by the hellish creature. All the neighbors still think the "Gringo es Loco." The younger children just look at me and giggle hoping for a rerun.

My previous chapter on winged wasps stands on its own. God used them to drive out the Philistines of the old bible lands. I am so glad I serve Jehovah.

Cockroaches just become part of life. When you live in the Jungle, it's just a given you're gonna do battle with the insect world. You win some, You loose some. After a while you kind of declare No Go Zones, and try to keep No Mans land to a minimum. Tupperware is your best defense. Cockroaches love electronics, they must like to listen to "tunes". You always find them inside your radio when changing the batteries. They love the cracks in your Books, Beds, walls, and you just can't live in a bubble. "Detente" is the term I used, can't live with them, can't live without them.

Beetles were always interesting, very few of them sting, bite or harm you, but they grow big and are they ugly, and stinky. The last beetle infestation we had was absolutely amazing. We had black beetles about the size of a quarter come out of the ground and during the night would be drawn to the lamplights. If you had an electric light it was like a black snowstorm. You could fill gunnysacks with them in the morning. They were very slow moving and nocturnal so they slept in daylight hours. During the day, they would crawl back into the ground or into your foam bed mattress. We could feel them crawling through our mattress after we had gone to bed, trying to dig their way out to fill the night with love and romance. It was a nuisance beyond belief, and by the millions, literally. The plagues of Egypt must have been so hellish. I don't know what part of the circle of life they belong to, but it can't be a good one. We spent weeks digging them out of our mattress and just when you thought you had them all out, another one would dig its way through, to wiggle between you and the sheets, and send you into another spasm of frantic digging, and ruining any romantic efforts.

So, to the scientist who study bugs and beetles and critters that crawl, fly, worm, wiggle, squirm, and dandle thru this earth, my hat is off to you. You are the stuff Hero's are made of. I, myself am

111

glad I have a can of Raid, and stock in the chemical companies who develop the cancer causing agents that delightfully decimate the enemy. May we all rest in Peace and give up the idea that the righteous shall inherit the earth, for we know it is not True... Insects RULE!

CHAPTER

18

O h! the Glories of a Song, whether sung in tune or out, is not important. The words and the meaning are locked in your head forever. Sometimes the place you first heard it, or the person you were with, sticks in your mind like a crab, crammed in a rocky cave of the sea, occasionally sticking its head out at the sight or smell of something of interest. I can definitely remember my first Jr. High School Sock Hop, when Three Dog Night, cranked out the song "Momma told me not to come". I was loving life till that song, and then all Mom's sermons came to haunt me and ruin the teenage desire of tasting the forbidden fruits. It was a love/hate relationship with that song from then on.

Cadence, rhythm, volume, tempo, or language is not of import either. No matter how awful life and the surroundings be, you can more than likely endure if you can open your mouth and sing, howl or growl. My life and its challenges were always softened, and gone through with a song. I grew up in church, and I mean literally grew up in church, and my greater part of musical impartation was gospel music. All other forms of noise were supposedly of the devil, and I was a willful participant in sinful recreation when apart from the church, but that was a rare occasion. I knew the Hymnal by memory from many a church. The verses that go to the songs were very familiar and especially the Pentecostal versions. I still love a four part harmony gospel quartet the best. Of course that category has to go to the Gaither families, Jimmy Swaggert's choir and those of that flavor. I went to a concert the Gaithers had in Fort Lauderdale where I now reside in the winter time and sang along with the other five thousand blue haired folks, and enjoyed every minute of it. We swayed and clapped and helped each other move our walkers and crutches from side to side, hoping our blood sugar and blood pressure levels weren't too high, from the emotion of it all.

Music and song were part and parcel of our jungle mission life too, and we sang through many, many
occasions and events. The ability to sing for hours on
end, and to stomp and clap till your fortified in the
"spirit" is definitely a positive for suffering whether
in youth, or old age. When all you have is memories
and the inability to go anywhere, you can always
reminisce and retrieve the depth of soulful Harpery
when you need it. I have a hidden tambourine that I
like to rattle on occasion. It's nice just to know that
the bangleling and pounding one can impart on a
good oiled skin, with a thumb that could shiver up
the face of a real skin tamberine is not a skill lost with
time. Black folk, or African-Americans can do things
with tambourines that us white, Euro-ungifted folk
even with years of practice long to do but alas, haven't the skills. After all the times I went to their
churches, danced and sang in the wondrously gifted
soul blessed, hat graced, high heel stomping good
times, I should be able to imitate some of their skills
but alas... I am unable to perform at their level. We
Pale Anglo folks are sadly unable to compete at that
level. Just like the Movie, "White Man Can't Jump",
White man can't tambourine either.

Some of the songs sneak back into my mind at
odd hours of the night. They even bringing back

the smells of the places I sang them in. Whether the church participants were white folk, colored folk, Indian folks, or Latino's. I know that some Political Correct folks will go nuts with the descriptions, but that was alright back when I was young. None of the people I went to church with were from Africa, nor did they desire to go to Africa. We even sang a song "Please don't send me to Africa". A ballad of expressed fear that God might call one to the mission field, and that we would go anywhere except Africa. Not that there's anything wrong with Africa besides the Malaria, Beri beri, TseTse flies, Man eating Lions and Hyenas and Ebola virus. In truth its probably a wonderful place. Anyhow none of my dark skinned brothers were Black back then, they are all varying shades of brown, and I was best friends with many of them. I have met a few that were even kind of blueish tinged, and that made it even harder to switch to the word "Black". I like the discarded word colored. As I work on my tan I am trying hard to become colored, but alas with great difficulty its not happening. I am like a barber pole, red to white, white to red, not much color in between.

I hate the division that has come into our lives because of Political Correctness. I think music blinded me to color and for that I'm grateful. I felt the same with the Sioux Indians I went to church with, sang with, danced with. I dislike the use of "Native American". I am native American, born here, raised here, parents from here, grandparents, from here. As a child I was taken to the Sioux Reservation in Montana, near Custers Last Stand, to a big campmeeting. I was thrown into the Little Big Horn river by some friendly Indian kids. They figured this was how you learn how to swim, and I almost drowned. Heavy drums beat, and electric guitars hammered out a rhythm that Black foot and Yellow foot musicians stomped in time. Cowboy boots on sawdust flooring under the big Revival tent made you dance all night. Maybe not so much moved by the Holy Ghost but by the awesome music they hammered out while getting in the "Spirit".

I so wish I could play an organ like the brother that fills the background for T.D Jakes as he rolls through his oratory and makes me want to jump and shout. The Latino beat that moves in our present church, makes me want to shuffle and shake my body too, but it will just not come naturally to me. I'm stuck with the so called "white guy" stiff marching band beat four/four time. It was drilled

into me as I practiced eight hours a day in prepa-
ration for the Rose Bowl Parade I marched in.
Along with a hundred other teenagers that I would
consider more on the pinkish side, than white, we
drilled till we dropped. We blasted our hearts out
to John Philip Suza, "March Grandioso". Eight
steps to five yards, knees waist high.

My musicianship started on a metal clarinet in
the fourth grade. When I opened it up for the first
time, the case exuded a dank smell of old spit, cork
grease, and metallic pocket change. Like pennies
that rubbed together left black greasy oil on your
hands. I suppose it was the cheapest instrument
known to mankind and left over from the inven-
tion of instruments, still in active use. It definitely
would have fit in the biblical category of a Sacbutt.
Through the years I graduated to a real wood clarinet, Baritone Sax, Tenor sax, I even played the
Cymbols. What a mistake that was, but I found that
music was part and parcel of my soul. Symphonic
Band, Symphonic Orchestra, Marching band,
and finally Jazz Band, where cool was cooler, and
"Wendi has Stormy Eyes" was the BOMB!

The guitar became my passion as I entered
the teenage years. The love affair with my first
Alvarez twelve string guitar swept me through the

Peter, Paul, and Mary age. The "Sounds of Silence" must have driven my parents crazy till a "Bridge over troubled Water" floated me out of the house. Nothing like a hormonal crazed teenager banging on a guitar to drive ones parents to make decisions such as "lets move to the farthest Jungle on the planet and disappear". Needless to say the clarinet was the first thing they made me leave behind. Leaving the guitar was not an option that I would even consider. My parents should give God the glory that we left before I could learn any of the New Age or Funk beats.

Once we arrived in the jungle, part of Mission Theology was to wake up at the crack of dawn and praise the Lord in Song. It takes some getting used to, but once in the groove you just kinda form the habit, kind of like coffee but without the coffee. We sang every morning at the crack of dawn, before we went to work. Songs like "We shall be changed" and "Libre, Libre" were staples of communal life. Around eight o clock after we had breakfast we would sing again. This time with a little more fervor since we had been worked up into a sweat out in the fields, " I will rejoice" and "Go get ready" were in the playlist. We could do a little clapping and a few gusty amens were slipped in behind the songs to show that we were changing and getting ready. It would be a hot day and a lot had to be done between now and lunch time. No way could we let the devil get a foothold in our thoughts.

Lunch time rolled around and while we waited for the steaming hot Sancocho to be served we could get in another great tune that always dispelled any weariness or complaints. "We give thanks" and then "On to Calvary" made the trek back out to the Fields where many a torturous adventure lay in wait, seem like it was easy.

Usually by late afternoon the heat, haze and mugginess of jungle life would overcome the ability to sing and it just became a contest of the will to make it through another day. By afternoon it was sheer endurance, another gallon of lukewarm Molasses Water, glugged down in hopes to keep dehydration and Sunstroke to a Minimum. The song "My hopes are built on Nothing Less" was not going to squeak out except under duress. "I shall not be Moved" was the theme song after four o'clock. As we walked in from the Fields, " The Move is on" would have risen from our parched throats if we had the strength.

Dinner at six, as dusk descended into darkness with a crash, always left that tune "This little light of mine" a good one to try and get us ready for church that night. A strident version of "We come together" would lift us back onto the path we had started out on in the wee hours of the morning.

We would then have an evening service where a rousing hour of song would end with "We shall be Changed".

I had an Alvarez twelve string guitar which made it hard to keep in strings. The jungle humidity would rust them out so fast that they would constantly break. I used to walk down the path to church for an hour strumming and humming, till I got married and had to carry the baby, and her diaper bag. Life never was the same again but the song "There is a Path which no Fowl Knoweth" still erupts every once in a while.

You had to be there to understand.

The craziest song I remember playing, was for my brother Patrick's wedding. We sang "Christ was born to Die". I played a Saxophone solo in the middle of the Mournful song, and was wondering how this happy event was going to turn out. The Poor guy never had a chance, as he and his bride both dressed in White stood together and smiled for the camera. Sorry Bro!!!He's a great guy when you get to know him, His ex-wife was awesome too. The relationship was doomed from day One, I think, because of the sad song. If you get asked to sing at a wedding pick something happy, please! Something like "Joy to the World" or "We wish you a Merry Christmas". I wish I had picked a different song now after all these years of thinking about it.

I love music, always have, always will. I like it all. Classical, Jazz, Symphonic Orchestra, Rock, Country, Marches, Salsa, Meringue. I love it all, and if I don't have an instrument, a pair of sticks or spoons will work just fine. I wore out a great guitar, and nursed many a metal string through hours of play. One of the most precious things back in those jungle days was to get a new set of guitar stings from someone in the mail. Oh! that was a great day. The ones you took off were oiled and saved in a cedar box so if you were in need you could reuse them.

They also made great leader wire when fishing for pirañas. Singing while fishing was frowned upon and not allowed, though a few shouts were permitted if shocked by an electric eel or stabbed by some horned creature of the deep that science has yet to name.

The jungle folk give the common title of "bicho", to these creatures. Translated it sort of means

"IT" or Dang Thing! It depends on how bad it hurt you or scared you. There are a lot of bicho's in the jungles of the Caqueta. If any of you reading this are interested in Biology, Etymology, Zoology or Bichotomy your fame is only an adventure away. Most of the time the creatures come looking for you. Be forewarned though, most discoveries of these unnamed creatures involve pain, and the song that comes to mind will probably intone like this oldie goldie, "When I get a touch Lord, from You".

CHAPTER

19

---~__~--

House building is an interesting topic to discuss with my newest Son in Law. He is an Engineer with Degrees I cannot pronounce much less understand. He has studied for years and could build anything to withstand everything, except the Day of Wrath promised in the book of Revelation. As a teenager, I had no such luck or training. A semester in Jr. High school shop where I built a B grade birdhouse was a start in construction skills, but I still needed a place to escape from my parents. The little bamboo box we were living in was getting smaller by the day. My brother and I were not getting along too well either, as the little bed we shared got hotter and smaller every night. The little bed being covered in a mosquito net that seemed like an oven lid when it was lights out, didn't help the scenario. We tussled and fought over every square inch. We quietly tried to kick each other out of the bed with out waking Mom and Dad, who slept twelve inches away behind the split bamboo partition, hearing us and getting all riled up. Nothing like having Dad stick his head over the partition and threaten bodily harm and a possible extra work detail the next day to put a stop to the problem.

Thanks to help from the Native Colombians I embarked on a great career of building every house I lived in and many others over the next fourteen years. The best instruction came from the most colorful of the congregation who I will call Indio Seraf. Seraf was the only real Colombian Indian I personally knew and was probably the most amazing man on the planet. He possessed talents no one else had. One of them as mentioned in a previous chapter was to tame Wasp. He could also do this with snakes. He never played with them but he knew how to see them, kill them, avoid them, make them be still. He knew how to hunt, fish, work and always had a smile on his face. He knew which trees birds nested in and soon provided a baby Parrot to my brother. We named the parrot "Peckwecka" which translates into the word "ToeJam". It was the only word he ever repeated, over and over. Most Parrots have huge vocabularies, and will sing and repeat the most amazing things. We had a neighbor, who's parrot would call the Hogs, Yell at the husband, Yell out the kids names, but ours alas, had only one word. The trauma of being raised by folks who didn't understand Spanish was just too much for the creature and he must have been so confused that he just decided to keep it simple.

Seraf lived with a dark eyed, bronzed skinned, fiery young lady, with gold flowers engraved in her front teeth. She was a small girl that could run down a jungle path and leave you in a cloud of dust. She was like a whirlwind who could make you cry if you tried to keep up with her while beating and dehusking a bowl of rice. She was twice as strong as any of us Americans, and was extremely temperamental. Seraf was not always so jovial when around her, and I think she was the only thing he was leery of, which was probably good judgement on his part. His teeth were the whitest Ivory and his hair jet black, straight cut in the bowl style you see in a National Geographic. He took us hunting one pitch black starless night and was able to traverse through the jungle without a flashlight. He was like a human submarine with onboard radar through the pitch black jungle. While I bumped into trees, stumbled into potholes, twisted into vines and long weeds, he smoothly sailed thru the night, gliding on silent feet, that moved with incredible swiftness. He would turn and hiss at us to be quiet, whereupon we would stop, swatting and smacking at the unknown things we disturbed in the dark. We were terrified that he would leave us lost in the jungle, which was to his delight. He would disappear, and reappear after our moments of terror and sobbing. Our desperate whispers of terror which would soften his merry heart, and he would reappear behind a tree right beside us scaring us even worse. It was rumored that his parents were witchdoctors and that was why he was so gifted. He sang "I've been redeemed by love Divine" in church services with the rest of us, so we overlooked the possible fault and we were grateful for all he did and taught us. He could make axe handles and boat paddles, with just his machete and a tree trunk pieces. He could carve out a dugout canoe with axe and adze and it would be a work of art. He knew which vines to pull out of the jungle to make baskets and how to weave them. He knew every tree and what its use was.

127

He could find little things to eat in the middle of plant clumps and nuts off of Palm trees that you could make a drink that tasted like hot chocolate. He was the only person I ever knew that could find the great big grey earth worms, one inch thick and ten inches long called "capitanas" for fishing. He would stand still out in the banana patch, with a shovel in his hand, then as if he could hear them, or feel them under his feet, turn to a certain spot and start digging like a dog. In a flurry of dirt he would have a huge worm in his hand.

Seraf helped me and my younger brother Patrick build our first house. We had nothing but our hands, and a borrowed hammer, an axe, and desperation to escape the breadbox we were living in with Mom and Dad.

Off to the Jungle we went, where we cut down our first "cerumbo" trees and begin to strip off the bark. The bark stripped off in long easy strips and these strips we used for rope, to tie all our beams and rafters together. The bark while fresh was strong and green, supple and easy to use. Once it was tied into place it would dry out and tighten into an unbreakable rope. The "cerumbo" poles as they dried out became light and hard, and made great rafters and lodge poles.

Bamboo which grew in huge clumps of thorn filled bunches was the next item in demand. Bamboo is the worst and best plant on earth. It grows up to six feet in a day. Up in the top of the bamboo you see small openings and I soon found out that big hairy tarantulas lived inside the bamboo. I used to break out in a sweat at the words "lets go cut down bamboo". I was terrified that the spiders would jump out and attack us. It took a while to realize they were just as terrified and would dive inside the bamboo to hide from us. I lost a lot of sweat just looking at the bamboo patch. There must be hundreds of different types of bamboo, but the one we used was the biggest, harshest, thorniest and strongest. It's hard to believe you can make sheets and clothes, out of house building materials, I can't imagine what processes it takes to do that.

We took the big bamboo and used the lowest and biggest parts for house posts. The middle parts for splitting into flooring and wall covers, the top part as lodge poles and rafters. We even made a ladder and stairs from the bamboo. Not one piece of the bamboo went to waste. You can take the very tips of the plant and invert them and use them for coat hangers and hooks for hanging pots and pans. I even made a knife for shucking corn out of bamboo. The edges of a split bamboo is like a razor blade, many a nasty knuckle gash was garnered as we worked long sweaty hours, splitting and cleaning the bamboo slats. I even carried a few of the long thorns that broke off in my foot for years. A nasty souvenir that tormented me every step I took, till they were removed by an ancient trick of stabbing the area with a hard object, making them fester and work their way out of your skin. Caquetanian bamboo is covered in toxic cilia. The itchiest, sliver like hair that covers its surface comes loose as you carry it. It gets ground into your clothing and skin, like glass shards. The long shafts of bamboo are covered in long, steel hard, tendrils that have one inch long thorns that are also covered in the same cilia. You have to learn how to weave your way through the patch and cut the tendrils at an angle so that your machete doesn't break. If you hit them straight on, at the base where they connect to the stalk they are so hard it will break your machete. Seraf, one of our first guides into the world of bamboo, tried to tell us all this, but our limited language skills and our total ignorance of bamboo harvesting was too much for him. He essentially had to do all the work and relegate us to draft horse duty. He cut the bamboo down, and we slowly carried it out, back to the homestead.

He then took us to a part of the jungle where a plant called "Iraca" grew in huge clumps and showed us how to cut this big leaf, pair it and weave it. It took fifteen thousand leaves to make our roof. During the effort we steadily continued in the draft horse duty. He was so fast and efficient that he could cut and fold the leaves faster than we could carry. The man was a machine and we were as inefficient as any greenhorns could be. Once the leaf had been piled and cured for two weeks we began to weave it onto the roof. Seraf was a phenomenal engineer and I'm not sure if he even knew how to read. What was unforgettable was spending the first night in a house I built with my own hands. The smell of curing bamboo, and Iraca leaf as it started to dry and shrink into the waterproof mat that was so cool in the hot afternoon. My brother Patrick and I, felt like we were ready to give up our tree house dreams as we slept that first night in the house that we built. Mom and Dad were excited too! The rumbling in the night was attributed to a thunderstorm up in the mountains.

CHAPTER
20

~ - ~ _ ~

Sharps, is a word used professionally for anything that has an edge, and especially anything with sharp edges. As a child, I guess I grew up in a totally sharps free environment because I never remember being cut, or bleeding. I'm sure I did, but nothing that was memorable, and probably because I never had a pocket knife. A word of wisdom to those who are city slickers, don't deprive the kids of sharp objects. You never know where they will go, and what they will do in life and you don't want them to learn the hard way like I did. Give them a pocket knife and teach them how to use it, unless you are a wussy type and don't know how to use them either. If so then you should just retreat into your cave and starve to death. Real

life in the Jungle is definitely survival of the sharpest, and it is either cutting you or you are cutting it.

Once I arrived in the jungle I bled a lot. I usually had a nice ugly scar to brag about after the
cut healed. A trophy to my manhood and sharps
educational failures. I think I cut myself on a daily
basis for the first year. I spent every day swinging
a sharp machete all day long and used it for everything from cutting fingernails, to digging for
worms. A knife or machete, is a tool just waiting
for you to find a use for it. Unfortunately skin is
not very forgiving and looses every time to a sharp.

I bought my first knife, a bone handled
Solengen German steel creation at the Army
Surplus Store. It smelled of neats foot oil, old rubber gas mask, fish eggs and musty old wool jackets
left over from the Korean wars. Before we left the
United States I visited this wonderland of Jungle
gear, and made my first sharps hardware purchase.
I was never allowed to even display or handle my
new acquisition till we arrived in the jungle. I had
hidden it amongst my precious things. As any good
reader of Edgar Rice Bourroughs, "Tarzan", we
know he depended on the long wicked implement
for Jungle survival and would never be caught
without the worthy tool of death. I had picked out

133

the best blade and bone handled scimitar I could imagine ever owning. I dreamed of using it to impale wild creatures of the deep dark Amazonian forests. Wielding it with great gusto in defense of life and limb, skinning the wild beast I would encounter and then cutting chunks of the delicious broiled meat that would be slowly turned on the brazier of my imagination. That knife became worth its weight in gold by the attention it garnered every time I displayed it, but alas it was a two edged sword. Unfortunately I had no idea how to use it and began to whittle away at myself like a crazy cartoon character that would have made Gepeto envious. For those of you who do not know who Gepeto is, he was the wood carver that made Pinnochio. I was Gepeto in reverse. Every time I unsheathed that knife I cut myself. My Colombian brothers had sharpened it up for me, and the old saying that a dull knife is the most dangerous, went by the wayside. I gave a new meaning to being "stuck like a pig".

There is a sensation that is hard to describe when you cut yourself. I remember it always happened so fast, and unexpectedly. I was always surprised, and it was over before it happened. It wasn't like the movies, slow and drawn out with a skittering violin screeching sound. It was more like a jolt of low volt electricity, sudden and jumpy. It was accompanied with a sour adrenaline taste in your mouth and a rush of sweaty queasiness. A flight of thought, should I scream or groan? A frantic flailing of the wounded appendage, as if trying to keep it from spurting blood that would seep out anyhow if you didn't move fast enough. Then the burning sensation that was searing thru your forehead like a thought of panic, is it bad? is it deep? why am I bleeding? will I die? how can I be this dumb to let the object I have in my hand, hurt me again? It took a while to figure out that you can look cool just having it on your belt, and it won't cut you if you keep it in the case. My Tarzan skills were slowly learned and painfully earned. Luckily I never lost any fingers, though it was a close call.

One of the first bad gashes came from trying to open a Cocao pod. I was taken on a trip to harvest logs for the sawmill, and while scrounging around the forest and making a general nuisance of myself, one of the young fellows that was on the trip showed me a tree with small green football like objects, hanging off the bark. He kept repeating the word "chocolate" and gesturing at these appendages. I love chocolate and was really excited at the thought of a candy bar hanging off a tree. It was kind of like the Garden of Eden, for a teenager, craving a MilkyWay, or Snickers. I whipped out the wondrous knife of Glorious renown, and began to try to extract this "chocolate". I first encountered that a Cocao pod is not that easy to cut open. They are easier to open by grabbing two of them and cracking them hard against each other, like big thick eggs. Once they are cracked open the white interiors are exposed, and you see a gooey white substance that is coating, what looks like huge kernels of brown corn. Disappointment was rising in my soul, since no Hershey's or AlmondJoy substance was to be seen. The young fellow who had got my hopes up began sucking on the white gooey substance that enveloped the big kernels. He was still smiling and repeating the the same words, "chocolate", pointing at the brown kernels again. I slurped a few kernels in and was not impressed. It didn't taste like chocolate to me. It tasted more like a sourish, sweet goop that should not be swallowed. After masticating the loose goop off the kernel my friend spit out the bare brown kernel, and repeated, "chocolate". By now, my disappointment was turning to irritation and despair. He then communicated somehow to me that inside

the kernel was "chocolate". Finally the heart of the
issue was at hand and within my grasp. The kernels
were too hard to bite through so I unsheathed the
awe inspiring knife. I commence to cut this unknown"chocolate" in half, to get to the expected
soft centered joy of delights. Unfortunately to my
great dismay, the slippery kernel was not coopera-
tive. While using extreme pressure to cut into the
kernel I slipped and gashed my index finger from
one side to the other. I could see exposed bone,
skin, tissue, weird looking white stuff and and lots
and lots of blood. I yelled and squeezed and bled,
till one of the guys came over to explore what the
ruckus was all about. He laughed and raised the
knife above his head and displayed it to everyone around. I was so confused, I am dying from a
mortal wound and chocolate withdrawal, and he
thinks this is funny? He grabbed one of the big
green leaves we had cut down and begins shaving
it down to a thin flat strap. He then slowly and
carefully wrapped my finger in a bandage like way.
The acidic taste in my mouth resolves into just a
gnawing pain, and slowly recedes into the sensation of disappointment. The knife is slowly and
with a new respect returned to its sheath on my
belt. The coolness and awesomeness of wielding

such a weapon has retreated into fear and embarrassment. I go back to the chocolate tree and its disappointing fruit, and see that I had been able to open the kernel, only to expose a hard green interior. As I nibbled on the kernel I was again disappointed to realize it tasted like a uncooked bean and had no "chocolate" flavor. It was only years later that I learned the secret of the Cacao tree, its Pods and how through much labor and processes it becomes what people know as "chocolate".

My finger was never the same, I had severed all the nerves and still have no feeling to the end of it. I'm lucky it healed and did not rot off. I did learn from the medical crash course, how to make band-aid material from the leaf, and used it frequently as I was a slow learner on the correlation of knife versus skin. The best day of my life was the day I dropped my knife in the river trying to skin a fish. Probably saved a few more of my digits from abrupt removal and mutilations.

Grass is a wicked sharp item. The Sawgrass that was like a million razorblades raking your arms and hands, or the Gigantic grass that was like the sharpest spear you could impale yourself on. Grass, no matter what type was always something to be aware of. May the Lord help you, if you grab a long blade of grass and let it slide in your hand or between your fingers. Many miserable nights were spent with these cuts being treated with disinfecting concoctions, that always burned sharp as a blade.

Splitting bamboo is a necessary survival skill. It is also a skill that without familiarity with "sharps" should be avoided. Bamboo has an outer shell that when opened and split, is razor sharp. When you spend a large amount of time splitting bamboo, you are sure to acquire a few choice cuts that will make you wonder, why you would ever need to buy a knife to injure yourself.

Eventually you learn to avoid the sharp edges of small things but with daily usage of your most valuable tool, the machete, it has to be earned. This was a battle I lost for a long time. I have more nicks and cuts than a ten pound slab of bacon.

While I was learning how to deal with sharp objects and how to avoid loosing fingers, we had a Jaguar roaming the neighborhood, raiding the pig pens, and hen houses. The family and neighbors were all on high alert during the nights. You would hear the pigs screeching and running out of their pens and out from under the houses, where they slept in the warm dust. The hair on the back of your neck would stand up on end when the screaming of the jaguar attacking sounded, while the pigs tried to escape. For all our efforts, we were never able to see the big cat during its attacks. It was the dark of the moon, and the cat was hunting every night. Some of our neighbors had come to sit through the night hunting the animal, but never could get sight of it. When you cannot see the thing you fear, it makes it scarier than it really is. The way it was described and hauled off our pigs, you would have thought it was the size of a Grizzly bear.

One night I had to go down to a neighbors house to put the chickens away in the hen house. His place was about a twenty minute walk through the jungle and banana plantations. On the dark of the moon nights, the spiders weave webs thru the jungle to catch the flying insects. All the way down the path to the neighbors farm, the spiders were out slinging webs. As I hustled down the path, I kept running into these webs. Unfortunately I decided to hold my machete out in front of me at arms length, to knock down the webs. Supposedly I would not be enmeshed, attacked and eaten by the huge spiders. I was holding my flashlight in one hand, and with the other hand my trusty machete, cutting through the webs. Holding it out

in front to brush the spider webs out of the way
I figured I was safe. Alas the consequences were
tragic at best.

The fear of a Jaguar on the roam in the dark,
with shaky shadows of big leafy banana plants as
they bristled in the wind, was making me sweat.
Panicky with fear, along with the evening heat and
enclosed jungle where plants grow thick and tall,
I was almost to a run. My fear had pushed me to a
point where I was not paying a lot of attention to
the path itself. When a shadow and rustling leaf,
brushed me from behind, I accidentally shook the
flashlight to create a jiggly figure of imaginative
terror. I tripped and fell, slashing my arm with my
machete in three different places. I am now bleeding, sweating, shaking in terror and still a long way
from a place of safety. I was really wishing I had
another hand to hold my trusty knife. I turned tail
and headed for the house, flashlight held in my
mouth, the biggest gash in my arm held shut by
one hand and my web sweeping machete in the
other. "Sharps" are hard to avoid when running
from Jaguars in the dark, with spiders chasing you.
I was thinking, to hell with the chickens. They
would have to deal with the jaguar on their own. It
turned out that night, the Jaguar was busy crawling

under my friends house, where he and his wife and baby decided it was time to have a noisy musical rendition of the chorus " The king is coming!". We woke up the next day missing another of our pigs, a lot of bandages, and a lot of blood spread around under my friends house.

A week later, a neighbors dog ran into the Jaguar and was able to tree it, and the neighbors shot it. Of course it was butchered and skinned, and photographed for posterity bragging rights. We were offered some of the carcass to divide up and cook, to replace our lost pork, not that it was a good tradeoff. We tried to make a meal out of it, but as you can imagine, cat meat is definitely lean and and should be left for the fantastic chefs from the other side of the world. No offense intended to the Asian community, but I wasn't impressed. Just so no one thinks we took joy in killing a cat, he was a mean one, and we were hungry, and fair is fair.

I didn't get to use my knife on him, but after all, I still have the scars to prove my valor. I could have made up a great big whopping lie about how I got clawed while fighting him in a hand to claw and fang fight, on that fateful night. I have the scars and could have showed the cuts as claw marks, but I'll just stick to the truth. I cut myself in three different places, with one stroke of the machete. A hand to hand fight with a jaguar, would have made a better story but I suppose this one, will have to do. Please pass me another Steri-Strip.

CHAPTER

21

I have met her, and I cannot sleep. I don't know who she is, I don't know where she lives. I wouldn't have a clue how to communicate with her. She was there at a distance, and I heard a voice I did not recognize, and poof, she was gone. What in Gods glorious creation was it that I had seen.

That was the end of my adolescent thought processing. It was her, the "One", the creature that defied description to anyone except myself, and man oh! man, I had no idea of how to obtain the impossible dream.

I had become a beast, a hormone addled human with one goal in mind. Pursuit at any cost, at any time and no barrier would deter me. I mean absolutely no barrier, and many there would be. I had seen and heard the stories of death defying feats for love, the romantic stories. All tales of lust and desire, fraught with situations of peril and difficulty, would not compare to the truth. Let me just say, at this juncture Truth is more bizarre than fiction.

I had encountered a young lady, a jungle princess. Many had cast an eye on her, and with a cat call whistle to attract and catch, had been quickly shunned. She was protected and guarded in a close knit home, on an Island surrounded by a river full of piranha, electric eels and other unknown species of pain inflicting creatures, I would pursue her till I made her mine.

If I had known how hard it was going to be and how long it would take, I probably would have stuck to the original plan, of turning eighteen and returning to the good ole U.S.A. to chase skirts unknown. I guess the mystery and intrigue of pursuit, finding a creature formerly unknown to me was the hook being set. I was a slack jawed, mouth breather, and had no chance at spitting the hook out. There was no turning back for me, as the days turned into weeks, months and years, I was hooked.

If my memory serves me right I saw her strolling down the path, on the way to church. She doesn't walk, she strolls. Slow and deliberate, queenly. Her gait is small and tight, she is short and crisp, demure and definite. She is wearing pony tails, long black tails, that hang down her back and remind me of every fairytale I can think of, mixed together. Her hair hung down to her waist and I would stare at it in the picture she one day gave to me. I still have the picture of her at the age of fifteen, posing with the luscious locks, and demure smile. She has high cheek bones, a nice chin, a small nose and eyes that are, well I don't know how to describe and cannot, till way later, in the discourse. I was not able to get close to the creature of my dreams for quite a while. All I could do is drool, and try to learn how to roll my rrr's so I could pronounce her name.

I learned from one of the guys across the river that her name was Rubiela. He had formerly pursued her but was shunned as a local, and she was unapproachable, because of family defenses. He didn't warn me of the four brothers, the father, the dog, and the castle defenses in place. He was kind enough to tell me she was a good catch, and good luck with the chase. He also helped me with the pronunciation issue, I would have.

You have to roll the "R" on the tip of your tongue. That is the way it is pronounced and it is a difficult name. "Rubiela" is an exotic name that gives any hormone addled adolescent an additional challenge to ruminate. Ruby Ella but with a rolled "R". The name takes on a sound that is totally different when pronounced correctly. I have to practice it a lot, and it never sounds right to me unless she says it. When she does, I cannot catch the meaning, except to hang slack mouthed in wonder. She told me later that her brothers thought I was missing a few screws and couldn't understand why I stood around with my mouth open like a fish out of water. It took a lot of years to convince them I wasn't dumb and could actually breathe through my nose.

I didn't know it at the time, but the tone and timbre of her voice is what sticks in my soul. After forty seven years, her voice has been an attribute that has held my attention when other things didn't. She is not melodic nor sonorous, but the tone was so in tune with my soul that I was left with a ringing sound in my mind that could not be stopped. Never has, Never will.

She is the eleventh child in a family of twelve. Six of her older siblings passed away as young children. One of them a baby girl who also had her name. She was her daddy's favorite and if I had known, I would have been wise to disengage my interest as soon as it started, but ignorance is bliss. I embarked on an adventure of romantic pursuit that would take three years to complete.

I was only sixteen when we met, and though I thought I was mature and ready to marry, I should say I am lucky it took a while to get through the process. In old pictures, I look like I am twelve, so thin, young and dumb, and of course most of the time with my mouth hanging open, like the mouth breather her brothers thought I was.

I didn't know it at the time but she was only thirteen when I met her. She looked older and acted older because her family upbringing was rather severe and reserved. She did not have much of a childhood, as I was to learn later, and was rather stoic and quiet. She was raised working hard and very protected, rarely to leave the farm she was born on and lived her whole young life. She really did live on an Island that was naturally cutoff from most of the world. She also had four brothers who's only job seemed to be to keep me from accessing her glorious presence.

A local custom on the river is if you hear someone holler from the other side of the river and wave, you hop in your canoe and go get them, as a courtesy. Kind of like stopping for the guy who's out of gas and blown a tire, with the hood raised on the side of the road. Also because you don't get very many visitors or people who come by, its a great time to have a visit, a way to catch up on the grapevine gossip. Maybe share a bowl of "cheecha", fermented juice that is fizzy and alcoholic in nature, and of course leads to telling even more gossip.

No such luck for the crazy Gringo from the mission, who frantically waves and yells and hand signals his desperate desire to get the other side of the river where the Princess of his dreams lives. Nope, it is not happening if any one of the four brothers has his way. All of the sudden it is time to get out a guitar and start up a lively song which gets the dogs stirred up, howling and barking. All of the sudden it is time to call the cattle in for milking, and to start the shrill yelling sound of STUUUUU...STUUU... calling in the hogs for feeding time. Nothing like a shooting match with muzzle loaded rifles, out in the backyard to distract from the skinny, ragged clown dancing on the other side of the river. No sir, nothing like it.

After a few sorrowful Saturday afternoons of defeat, I decided that if Tarzan could out swim a few fat lazy gators, I should be able to do the same. I ran into the banana patch, stripped down naked and stuffed my clothes in my boots. With one hand I held the boots out of the water and with the other I swam across the river. I jump up into the bushes and sawgrass on the other side, to unpack my clothes and hurriedly dress as best I could while drip drying. Do you realize how hard it is to swim with one arm, holding your boots up out of the water, against the current, on the lookout for Gators, snakes or anything else that could look at a naked, pale, moving object as lunch? I was lucky in the endeavor, as no creature of the lagoon decided I looked tasty and worth the effort to eat. Even creatures of the deep can recognize a poor skinny specimen, with nothing but skin and bones. A crazy imitation Tarzan was not a target worth pursuit. Thus I escaped unscathed and intact.

After a quick inventory of body parts and realizing that all appendages were still attached I decided I would never be deterred again. It was not an easy feat, but no one could say I was a coward. Of course no one was watching for a naked pale skinny apparition, to pop out of the water. They were all out back shooting, singing and feeding the hogs. The problem seemed solved, except the damp bedraggled Gringo kept mysteriously showing up, without any help. Persistence is one of my attributes, and it probably wore the brothers down. They eventually just accepted the fact that no matter how ignored I was, I would show up. Just another stray animal to avoid and be wary of.

The next obstacle in this romantic pursuit to be overcome was desertion. I would show up and the only people in the house would retreat upstairs and I would be left downstairs the dog. "Compañero" was the dogs name and he never left my side while I visited. Mom, Dad, or cousin Rosita would come down from upstairs eventually and acknowledge my presence, and then retreat back upstairs. I would be left to hold a lonely conversation with the dog, for most of the afternoon. It was a long time before I was invited upstairs to sit on the porch, to be observed as some foreign invader, possibly to be removed by force, if the wrong move was made. I was very still.

I was terrified of her Dad, Don Chépe. All the people on the river called him this. His real name, only revealed after many years, was Jose Maria Henao. He was an honored citizen of the region and looked up to, by all who knew him. He was a stout heavy man. In a setting where most people are small, skinny and dark, he was very distinct. He always wore a Felt Fedora and a wool "Ruana" poncho style over one shoulder. It made him look huge and his voice was very gruff. He shaved once a week and his bearded stubble just added to the persona of "Dont mess with the Boss". He never really conversed with me but sort of hemmed and hawed a little as I would greet him. He was King of the castle and most of the neighboring jungle. I had been told through the grapevine that he was a tough guy and would never give his favorite baby daughter to anyone, much less a damp, skinny Gringo. It was going to be a challenge for sure.

Señora Rosanna was her mother, and God bless her soul, she was merciful to me and treated me like the castle fool. She would pour me a coffee and ignore my presence, and leave me to sit with one of the hunting dogs who took a liking to me. "Companero" was a golden short haired labrador who became my lovelorn hand holder. We sat for many hours downstairs, in the main room, while everyone who was able to make excuses for staying upstairs would avoid the damp suitor and the dog. Dogs of course are never allowed upstairs. Finally after a few hours, the Princess of the house who I had risked life and limb for a glimpse of, would slowly come down the stairs and briskly be whisked into the kitchen to prepare dinner for the uninvited guests and crazy Gringos who showed up. I would get glorious glimpses of her coming and going, while casting forlorn glances toward the kitchen. Pots and pans were furiously rattled around to make a showing of busyness that would discourage any intrusion by the skinny, opened mouth Gringo. It took a few months before I finally intruded into the kitchen and asked if I could help. Everyone in the family had their suspicions confirmed, the Gringo really was crazy...

Everyone knows real men don't go into the kitchen, Never! Ever!

Cousin Rosita was ordered to never leave the Princesses's presence and it was never any other way. She was a few years younger than Rubiela and was very quiet, so it never bothered our time together as little as it was. She stayed with us even after we were married, for years. Even the dog "Compañero" went with us. I won him over and no matter how many times the brothers came and took him back to the Island, he would show up at our house. Rubiela's brother who owned him said he would sell him to me, and I said no thanks. They would take him back home and Companero would be back at my house the next morning. Hahahaha! persistence pays off. I got the girl and the dog!

The brothers finally decided that I was not going to disappear, so they just tried to make the courtship as difficult and long as possible. They were probably hoping I would die from starvation, malaria or drowning, as I constantly crossed the river naked with one hand, holding up my boots and clothes. It wouldn't have been hard to assist in my demise with some assistance from the local witchdoctor, who lived on the other side of the river, where I started the naked river run. I eventually built my own canoe and didn't have to do the swim. I was was able to show up dry, without the fanfare, and it was obvious I just would not quit.

The kitchen was to be the scene of our courtship, and we were able to sneak a few kisses and "piropos".

Piropos are flirty looks of desire. You can get away with these when cousins and brothers backs are turned if you are quick.

We didn't get to converse a lot because I barely knew any Spanish and she spoke no English. Sign language, fluttering eyes, and sneaky hand holding are an art form which we became good at. We still love to hold hands and throw a few piropos and are no longer hurried about it.

I courted Rubiela for three years, and we married not only once but twice. Her father asked us to be married by the Catholic Church and we did. We then had a good old fashioned revival wedding at the Mission, three days later. Don Chepe wasn't going to attend the Mission Wedding, but I convinced him that his presence was needed. To give her away as my bride would bring great significance to his standing in the community and he acquiesced. He was a proud man and even if the crazy skinny gringo was pitiful, he was persistent. I worked on the mouth breathing, and believe that I have made him and his family proud.

I can thank God for the Princesses patient and slower paced character. It held me back from some of the crazy and frenetic actions I would have loved to have engaged in. I lucked out that she really was a total opposite of me. After forty seven years of being together, she is still my Princess. I have lost the skinny part, and the mouth breathing when she is looking at me. I am still a little crazy, energetic and persistent. My skinny dipping days are behind me, and I am now accepted by her family for what that is worth.

CHAPTER
22

All trips and stories come to an end, usually. Or they have sequels and comebacks, that bring the world they have introduced roaring back into the interested followers. I suppose I will see how this one sells and the interest it sparks. If you like it and want more, let me know. I will leave my email at the end of the story and we will look forward to hearing from you. Even if you dont like it, I will look forward to hearing from you. No, you won't get your money back, just donate the book to your nearest charity or prison. Someone more gullible than you might appreciate it, or use the pages to roll some cigarettes and smoke them. You think I'm kidding right? And of course there are the many in far away foreign

lands that need a page for cleaning the old derri-
ere, after a bout of amebic dysentery, or stomach
disorders that come from eating things that we're
not mentioned in this work of art. There are places
in this world where the leaves of the plants are not
usable, and contain poisonous cilia that leave painful results. I've been there and done that too. You
learn which plants to avoid for that usage, as well
as the slick pages of the old National Geographics
that just smear the results. Its worse than a hand
full of sand, a trick I heard of and tried..... once.....
and then you start carrying around crummy novels
to use page by page with much more appreciation.
Just ask the folks who suffered through the 2020
pandemic and its T.P. shortages. No tree was safe
from the destructive defoliating movements.

Writing a book is not as easy task. I hope that
my diction is as clear as my thoughts, it was not
easy trying to put them on paper. The imaginary,
the wishful, the truthful, the doubtful, the enhanced, the obscured, were all included with the
best intent to let the reader enjoy the experience.
It has been a three year project to do this and I am
spurred on by the desire to leave my grandkids the
memories and stories I have told them.

The smells, the colors, the feelings, the sensory jolts that occur during our life should be passed on to the ones we love. Hopefully it was a pleasurable read to the ones that do not know me, or are incapable of traveling to far off and diverse places. I am glad that I was taken on the life course that I passed through. I am saddened because I cannot take my grandchildren to the places where it happened. Due to political upheaval and the evil that occurs in our time, Socialism and Communism have destroyed the Colombian countryside and inflicted terror on the wonderful people I so love and miss.

I wonder as I pen these words what the future holds for so many that I love. I wish I could tell their stories, but cannot due to the conditions that have enveloped our world. We will miss out on so much that would leave us so much the better.

To all my friends and family that might construe themselves as part of this novel, thanks for being an imaginary part and I hope you enjoy this crazy world I remember and portray to the best of my abilities

To you of my family and children, hopefully this is a Novel you can read, remember and cherish knowing I had you foremost in my mind as I penned the pages and enhanced or obscured the facts.

I hope to pen some more as my years in Alaska also created the works of a novel that would be interesting too. Working in the Prison is all it was to be cranked up to be. What isn't interesting about Murder, Lies and Spying on people?. Alas the book can only be so long before people decide it is to big and heavy, and doesn't fit in a hip pocket for quick use. Hasta la Vista baby!!!I'll be back!!

ABOUT THE AUTHOR

Michael Holland was born in Denver, Colorado, in 1955. He went to the jungles of the Caqueta River, in Colombia S. America in 1972. He returned with his wife Rubiela, and three children to Colorado in 1986. Fluent in English and Spanish he interprets for public events. He moved to Alaska in 1988 and currently resides there with his wife and four grown children and seven grandchildren. Certified by Alaska Police standards counsel in 2001, he had a successful career in law enforcement, in Corrections and with the Federal Marshal Service. He retired from law enforcement in 2018. He attended the University of Alaska. He Received a Doctorate of Divinity in 2011 and Co-pastors churches in Florida and Alaska. He does public speaking, teaching, marriage seminars and translation services. For speaking engagements he can be contacted at **pto2holland@hotmail.com**

Michael's descriptive narrations paint pictures that were imprinted on his senses. Without documented proof of his experiences he turns his stories into Creative fiction to improve and capture his audiences, catapulting them into the amazing possibilities of laughing at life's crazy realities, and challenges. **If you enjoy the book let me know. I might start another one.**

THE BILLY JOE HOLLAND STORY

I, Billy Joe Holland, was born on September 26, 1936 about two or three miles west of Cherry Hills, Arkansas.

This little town is off the road to Mena, about a mile North of the old Coogan place. There was a wagon road up to the old plank house and the best I can remember it was four rooms with a big wide hallway between the two rooms on either side. I seems like the hallway was open on both ends. The old house was made of wood planks with a wood shingle roof. It had a front porch that went completely across the front of the house and there was a big cedar tree or two in the front yard.

I was born at that old house and I was told that Mandy Philpot, was the Midwife that delivered me. I have since wondered how she had gotten there in time, because the only way in was to walk, or by wagon or horseback and we had

163

neither. Dad would have had to walk to go get her, and probably both walked back and no one lived within probably close to a mile from where we lived. My first memories in life were in that old house back in the woods. There was a large field out front, it seemed like a long way across, but it was probably only a hundred yards to the edge of the woods, and down a small hill to the spring, where we had to carry water back to the house. Mom had her old wash pot down by the spring, for washing clothes. I remember her making hominy down there. I am not sure exactly how she did it, but I think it was by boiling corn in a big old ash pot they also used, to boil our clothes to get them partially clean. She would use the old scrub board to finish cleaning the clothes, She would then carry the clothes back up to the house and hang them out to dry on the clothes lines, my Dad had strung up for her.

Dad grew corn and sweet potatoes in the garden and in the field in front of the house, there was a trail down the middle that went down to the spring. There was an old well dug out to the side of the house, but it was boarded up and was dry. The closest water was in the spring, down under the hill.

When I was six years old in 1940, I think I heard some one say it was March 8th but I am not sure of the date. We were riding home from school on the school bus, and we saw a large plume of smoke coming up, from back in the woods where we lived, and when we got off the bus we found out from the people who lived there, that our house was on fire. They would not let me go up there to see, but the old house burned down to a pile of ashes. The only thing saved was the clothes we were wearing. I was told later, while we as family were talking,that it was a spark from the old wood stove that blew out on the old dry wood shingle roof and the house went up like a match box.

It was said that at that time, Mom was pregnant with my sister Linda. Ruby was a baby, and when Mom discovered the house was on fire she started to run for help. Ruby was asleep on the bed and as Mom ran past the bed, Ruby woke up and Mom just reached out and grabbed her up in her arms as she ran by and headed down the trail. When everyone got back up there, nothing was left. I guess God was watching over Ruby, and made her wake up or she may have been lost in the fire. We, the children were sent to different peoples homes to stay, while Dad found another place to live. The people were so generous and gave what they could, and we set up housekeeping again at the Simpson place, which is now called the Barney place. I"m not sure but it seems like I heard from some where that they paid $5.00 a month for the rent. It was another old plank house with a wood shingle roof and large open hallways between the four rooms. It had a barn out in front, and by then we had gotten a couple of cows, and we had milk and butter. This place also had a big spring down the hill, and we had to carry water from it, and Mom again, had that big old cast iron washing pot that was used to boil clothes. This spring had a cement and rock pad around it, and it had the best and coldest water in the county. Dad made a wooden chute down below the spring and the cold water ran through it continually keeping our milk and butter cold. We kept the milk in gallon lard and syrup buckets. Every meal, we could go down the hill and bring up a bucket of cold milk and butter and water.

Dad was a Jack of all trades and did many jobs to make a living, but I remember mostly he shingled houses and barns and was known as a woodsman.

Dad cut timber all over the county, all that was in walking distance of four to eight miles from home. He could sharpen a cross cut saw that would sing like bird when you cut into a big tree and his ax could cut through a limb as big as your arm, with just one swing. Anytime there was a tract of timber to be cut, you could bet Dad would be one of the first people asked to do the work.

I was six when we moved into the old Simpson place, and my sisters, Myrtle, and Rosie were already married and gone. My brother Ervin left not too long after that, and I don"t remember him much.

I remember the first horse that Dad ever had. Her name was Pet, and she was about fourteen years old when we got her. Dad cut six racks of wood and traded that to Gus Hearn for that old Nag, but she served the purpose. Dad made a small two wheeled cart to use for hauling wood, and groceries and pine knots and such. It didn't have any brakes, but Dad had cut a sturdy hickory pole about the size of your arm and about eight foot long, and when we needed to slow the cart down on the hills he would just jam that pole down in front of the cart and pulled back as hard as he could. It was pretty primitive but it worked. Dad would ride her to Cherry Hills at times, to get flour and stuff and didn't have any trouble at all, but when one of us kids would try to get on and ride, she would just turn around and head for the barn. We would lead her down the road a ways, and find a high bank and jump on her back to go to Cherry Hill but she would just turn around, she would head back to the barn. If you fell off of her, she would stop and wait for you to get up and lead her off.

One time Dad had a big peanut patch. He was plowing weeds with her and he stopped to do something with the traces, and while he was bent over she crapped on his New railroad Cap. Well if you know Dad, he come up cussing and slapped her with the reins and she took off. He pushed the plow in the ground as hard and deep as he could, trying to stop her and she just kept going, him yelling and cussing. I think she plowed up an acre of peanuts before he got her to stop.

I remember in the summer when it would get really hot, that the house we lived in had a front porch that ran all across the front, and we would all pull mattresses off the beds, and set them on the porch trying to sleep in the cool air.

I remember lying under the big old black walnut tree there on lazy summer days watching the white clouds drift by and trying to make up my mind what they looked like. I could see elephants, whales, snakes and a variety of other things as they drifted by.

I remember going fishing with Dad many, many time on Saturdays and Sundays. We would fish in the little creeks and walk to the river and fish all day, coming home sometimes after dark, because we would fish until we caught enough for a meal or until it got sundown. When we got home and we didn't get enough Mom would say "My goodness they ain't enough here to make the grease stink." Well as you know back then, when you had fish for supper that's what it meant, you had fish and biscuits and that's all, nothing else. It took a lot of fish to make a meal. The same would apply with squirrels and rabbits, but then Mom would make gravy to go with the biscuits and squirrel's. If we didn't have enough squirrels and rabbits for a meal it wasn't unusual to pop off a few Robins or Woodpeckers to make enough meat for a good meal.

As time went on, we moved into the old Herman Eggen house and we had to walk to School as the bus didn't run by that house. By the way, when we lived at the Simpson place we only had to walk down the road about a mile to the road that went to Highland and we could catch the school-bus there. We would go barefoot as long as possible in the fall because you only got one pair of shoes a year, if you were lucky. They would have to last a really long time, so we would carry our shoes and walk down that road to catch the school bus barefoot and you would stub your toes on a rock and just peel the skin off the end of a toe..Oh how that would hurt and then when you had to put your shoes on it would hurt even more.

Anyway I was getting older and remember more of those years. We had hogs and cows and that old horse and chickens. We raised gardens, turnips and all kinds of stuff to eat plus Dad was also a great hunter, and alway seemed to have a good Coon hound around and in the winter months he hunted a lot. He could sell the hides from the coons, opossum, skunks and mink. A big coon hide would sell for five to six dollars and the possums for two to three dollars. Skunk skins were four dollars and minks were thirty to forty dollars. Dad would sell the hides just before Christmas so we would have a little extra money then.

About the time I was twelve or thirteen, Dad began cutting timber for Dart Mills, who had a saw mill. He decided he would up and move his was mill to California, and that left the 40 acres over by highland for sale. Dart Mills told dad he would sell him that forty acres for five hundred dollars, if he would agree to go to California and work for him. Dad decided that would be a good thing, to have his own place, no more renting. Dad went through with the deal and we moved again, over on the road to Highland. The old house was just a sawmill shack, and was built with semi green lumber, so when the planks dried out there were large cracks in the walls. It was only three rooms. The inside wasn't finished. It was just bare two by four studs. The outside planks were rough and as Dad would say with "cracks big enough to throw a cat through without ruffling the hair."

We moved in Mom, Dad, myself, my sisters, Ruby and Linda and Caroline. This was a good place because the school bus ran right out in front. No more walking to school. We didn't have electricity but there was an electric pole in the front yard. We still had to do homework with coal oil lamps and we got an ice box. The oldest Howard boy would bring us fifty pounds of Ice. Twenty five pounds would fit into the ice box, the other twenty-five pounds, we put in three washtubs, wrapped with an old quilt. We would use an ice pick to pick off Ice. The ice was needed for the ice Tea. Boy, was that something to have cold Ice tea for a meal or cold water just to drink.

We were really uptown now, cause Dad made pretty good money in California and sent money home so Mom would have a little money for stuff we needed. Willie Eiger, owned the gas station down the road and sold canned goods, flour, corn meal and such. We would charge whatever we needed, and when Dad sent money, Mom would pay part of what we owed. I don't think Willie ever got paid off completely, until Dad came home from California. He paid all the people we owed money too, and still had money left over, to get by on, until spring when he would go back to California to work.

Dad bought himself and I both, .22 pump action rifles and by now, I was big enough to go anywhere he did. and I was just like his shadow. I was always about ten steps behind him whether we were hunting or fishing, I was alway there and he was always talking, it didn't seem to matter if I heard or answered him, He just kept on walking and talking. We hunted those hills and mountains for several miles around that old house and I never knew of Dad ever getting lost day or night, except for one time. He and Ode Garmin went up on Shock creek, Coon hunting one night and it clouded up and they couldn't see the stars to know what direction they were going. They finally walked out of those mountains down by Pine Ridge about 9:00 am the next day, they caught a ride back to Cherry Hills. Never thought anything about it after that day .

Dad and I cut timber all over the country during those years, after he got the house paid off. He quit going to California and we just worked around home wherever there was timber needed cutting.

Gus Hoover had two old Dodge flat bed trucks and he would buy timber. Dad and I would cut it and he would haul it to Mena. We worked all over the country. We would walk to Cherry Hills early in the morning and ride the old truck where ever needed, and cut timber all day. Then we would ride back to Cherry Hills where Gus Hoover lived and we walked home every evening.

Some time later Dad decided to go back to California and work again. He was getting too old by then to work in the woods, so he worked as a night watchman at the saw mill.

In the meantime I had grown some and was old enough to work in the woods by myself. I kept working for Gus Hoover, cutting poles and pulpwood. Jimmy Bowling, myself and Russell Hoover who was Gus Hoovers oldest son, we worked together. Russell drove the truck and we there were like the three Musketeers cutting and hauling poles to Mena. Gus Hoover was real generous, he paid us twenty dollars a week if we could cut and haul two loads a day. We did, and always seemed to have enough money, so we could go to town on Saturday nights to the movies.

J.M. Martin lived up the road from us near Highland, his dad Marion Martin was a Bootlegger and sold moonshine. When things got rough in the moonshine business he actually would work in the woods cutting timber for a while. He was quite the fisherman. His niche was Trot line fishing for catfish, and he and Dad used to fish a lot together. They would camp out down on the river for a few days at a time. Mom wasn't too fond of that because Dad would always come home with a snoot full of moonshine. Marion was always drunk himself and Dad couldn't seem to say no when the jug was passed around.

Marion Martin had an old forty-six Chevy coupe, that he used to pick up and deliver moonshine in. Every Saturday, Marion would get drunk while selling his moonshine and when this happened, Jim his son, would take him home. On Saturday evenings he would ask to borrow the car and of course Marion, being drunk would almost alway say yes. So Jim, Me and Russ Hoover and Jimmy Bawling would go to town every Saturday night, to the movies and to drive main street all night. All four or five blocks of it, and then to the bus station for burgers and a Coke. It was the only thing open after 10:00 p.m. Boy, we spent many Saturdays nights doing that, as we grew up to be mischievous young men.

One time we went down to Roy Garrets place down on the river. He had a great swimming hole there, and we thought he had gone to town that day. He had a great big watermelon patch down in the field behind his house. He thought he had it hidden in the middle of his cornfield, but needless to say we knew where it was, and we proceeded to each take a watermelon, one apiece. J.M., Jimmy Russels, and myself, went down to the creek laying the melons in the water to get cool, we then had a great day swimming and eating stolen watermelons. Well, Roy Garret hadn't gone to town that day and was sitting on his screened in porch, watching us, as we crawled up through the corn patch, from stealing his melons, and as we opened up the gate to leave Roy yelled out "Hey! you boys can't come back to swim anymore cause I saw you stealing my melons! ". We all were riding bicycles and we took off like rockets, and never went back. Later, years after I was married and had gone back home to see Mom and Dad, my Dad and I were fishing down in that same hole of water, and Dad says to me, " Son I guess you know If I had found out about you boys stealing Roy Garrets watermelons back then I would have kicked your ass all the way down to his house and made you apologize to him".

Dad and I used to have lots of good times together. I was still just like his shadow, always ten steps behind him. We hunted Coons, opossums, skunks, all over those mountains and even down on the river. It wasn't nothing to walk down the river and hunt until two or three o' clock in the morning . We would then head back home, and most of the time we had a sack full of coons to eat. Mom could really make baked coon taste good, but were were used to eating those kind of things and was glad to get it.

As I grew up, we were always glad when some of the family would come back home to visit. It didn't matter who it was, we were just glad to see someone. I never really knew many of my family, except Ruby, Linda, and Carolyn, my sisters, the others had married and left home while I was still pretty young. As for the old house we didn't change it much. Dad finally built another room for a kitchen, after the first one almost fell down. We always had to carry water from the spring down under the hill. When I was fifteen, we finally got electricity in the house. Willie Egger wired the house, charged Dad Thirty dollars for the job. It wasn't much of a job, because he only put light in the ceiling of each room and couple of plug-ins in each of the other rooms, but we were so grateful for it. Now we could have a refrigerator, and light to do homework with. We even got an electric radio. Boy, we were really high class. We still had the all wood heater in the front room and a wood burning kitchen stove. We cut enough wood to Sink a battle ship, trying to keep that old house warm, and wood for Mom to cook on.

Mom was from a pretty well to do family, and she had her ideas on how to make that old shell of a house, look good inside. People would bring us old newspapers, mostly Aunt Bonnie and Aunt Ruby. They lived in Little Rock, and would save up old newspapers and bring them when they came to visit every few years. Mom would take those newspapers and make a paste glue from flour and water, then paper the whole inside of the house with clean news papers. We didn't know it then, but every layer of old newspaper would help as insulation and helped to keep the wind from coming through the cracks . I'll bet there are at least six to eight layers of old newspapers in that old house, but it served its purpose. It looked all clean, while it covered up all the old flyspecks and torn places and yellowed out, old papers.

We hunted and fished, cut wood and cut timber. Us kids went to school, and I finally graduated. I was the first child to actually graduate from High School, although some of the others did get their G.E.D. later in life. My eldest sister, Myrtle, went to college at the age of fifty and got a degree, and she taught third grade children for quite a few years.

I left home when I was seventeen, and went to Denver, Colorado. I married two times and had four children. I had three sons, and one daughter. Michael, Patrick, Jeff, and Pamela. At the present time of this writing, September of 2017, my second wife Mary Ellen and I will have been married 56 yrs. My first wife Colleen, was long ago and we did not last but five years. We have four children, ten grandchildren, twelve great grandchildren and two great, great, great grandchildren.

P.S. This history was given in handwriting to my Eldest son Michael, for him to transcribe off the handwritten account, in 2022. Maryellen has passed on this year and is sorely missed.

P.S.S. My father gave this story of his past to me, Michael, the elder son, to write and put in electronic forms so we could pass it on to the other kids and grandkids. I know my Grandson Weseley will enjoy this and I might try to put it in my own book if I ever get it finished...

Thanks Dad for sharing this ... ... May it be a small piece of history, from the backwoods of Arkansas, and the great country of the United States of America... God Bless all of my Family!

The Hollands..

Made in the USA
Columbia, SC
20 September 2023

23082062R00112